D0173479

Flyover Fiction
Series editor: Ron Hansen

It's Not Going to Kill You,

and Other Stories

Erin Flanagan

University of Nebraska Press | Lincoln and London

© 2013 by Erin Flanagan

Acknowledgments for the use of copyrighted material appear on page 193, which constitutes an extension of the copyright page.

All rights reserved
Manufactured in the United States of America

Publication of this volume was assisted by a grant from the Friends of the University of Nebraska Press.

Library of Congress Cataloging-in-Publication Data
Flanagan, Erin.
[Short stories. Selections]
It's not going to kill you, and other stories / Erin Flanagan.
p. cm.—(Flyover fiction)
ISBN 978-0-8032-4629-4 (pbk.: alk. paper)—ISBN 978-0-8032-4931-8 (epub)—
ISBN 978-0-8032-4932-5 (mobi)—ISBN 978-0-8032-4699-7 (pdf)
I. Flanagan, Erin. It's not going to kill you. II. Title.
PS3606.L356I88 2013
813'.6—dc23
2013005669

Set in Lyon by Hannah Baker.
Designed by J. Vadnais.

To Kelly Hansen

Contents

Acknowledgments

I'd like to express my gratitude to Yaddo, the UCross Foundation, and the Wright State University Department of English for their support and the time to write. Many thanks to the editors and staff at the *Florida Review, Prairie Schooner*, the *Madison Review, Lake Effect, Crazyhorse, Colorado Review*, and *Wag's Revue* for publishing my work and supporting writers. Thank you to Kristen Elias Rowley and the entire staff at the University of Nebraska Press, and to my agent, Gail Hochman, for her continued support.

Thanks to Sarah Twill for her great memory and the details for "The Winning Ticket," the title "The Summer of Cancer," and many side stories within the collection. Thanks to Brian Young for the story "All I Want Is You" and for living the air rock 'n' roll dream. Thank you to sticker group: Deborah Crusan, Lance Greene, Doug Lantry, Peggy Lindsey, Noeleen McIlvenna, Carol Mejia-LaPerle, Sirisha Naidu, Nimisha Patel, and Sarah Twill. Thank you to my family: Ken, Judy, Kelly, Doug, Andrew, Alicia, Ellen, and Neil. Special thanks to Mike for his support while writing this book and to Barry for help writing the next book. And all my gratitude to Cora for reminding me that writing comes from life.

It's Not Going to Kill You,
and Other Stories

It's Not Going to Kill You

Candace wonders which is a bigger sin: to take communion and not mean it or skip it all together, and if she doesn't believe in God, does it matter one way or another? What she does believe in right now is keeping the peace. Her mother, Laurel, taps Candace twice on the knee then stands with her crutch in her armpit. Candace follows obediently, knowing if she stays in the pew her mother will be angry, the rest of the congregation taking note. She makes her way sideways to the end of the pew, trailing her mother's staggering step to the front of the church, where Candace sticks out her tongue to receive the wafer from an eighth grader in a white robe. Candace saw this girl earlier as she was dropping Wally off in the children's room—her too-short plaid skirt, a mesh top over a black tank—but now in the robe the girl looks angelic, the only hints betraying her true self are the too-dark eye makeup smudged above her eyes, the red lipstick too yellow for her skin.

Back in the pew, the chalky wafer dissolved and stuck in the back of her throat, Candace fumes that she's already bent to the will of her mother. Laurel called on Thursday night and said she'd slipped in the bathtub—"Nothing too serious. When I came to, everything still worked."

"Came to?" Candace echoed and knew it was worse than her mother had let on, that she wouldn't be calling and *not* asking for help unless she needed it. Candace asked Rhonda Lantry to cover her shifts at the hospital—knowing Rhonda never did a favor for free—and pulled Wally out of school on Friday, telling the principal it was a family emergency and she didn't know when they'd be back. Saturday night when Candace arrived home, driving her Volvo down the long, rutted lane, she was surprised by her mother's appearance on the porch—her lined face, her white hair, an Ace bandage wrapped around her ankle, the leg unable to support weight. As a nurse, Candace could tell her mother had done the bandage herself, that the wrap was too lax and nearly useless.

"Nothing serious?" she said as she bent to hug her mother, and Laurel bucked away saying it's not like she cracked open her skull and to move out of the way so she can get a handle on that grandchild. Candace wondered if all this aging had happened since her father died or if it had been accumulating over the decades and she just hadn't noticed. Candace had promised her mother at the funeral that she would try to make it back every three months or so, but somehow a year has passed and she's just now returning. Each time she thought about it—the Fourth of July, Wally's birthday in September—she couldn't imagine coming home without her father—the quiet of the farm with no one there to mediate between her and her mother.

"I thought you were getting in a few hours ago," her mother said when Wally finally wiggled away. "I made beef stroganoff, Wally's favorite. It's a brick now thanks to his mom." And that's how Candace ended up in church, to pacify her mother. It's January, and she figures this is as good a way of celebrating the New Year as anything else: exchanging passive-aggressive lunges with her mom.

Candace feels a tap on her shoulder and turns to see the plump woman from the Sunday school room. "We've had an incident," the woman whispers, her eyebrows drawn together.

Candace glances at her mother, who hobbles behind her out of the pew, and the entire church watches until they're out in the hall. Wally is waiting for her outside the children's room, a stuffed Moses in his hand. He is a soft-looking child who wears clothes from the husky section, still years away from the growth spurt that will lengthen his body to proportion. He catches his mother's eye and sniffs heavily. Laurel gets to him first—even on one leg she's spry as a chicken—bends at the waist, and puts her palms against his chubby cheeks. "What happened?" she says. "God find out your mom's not a Christian?"

"Not exactly," the woman who pulled them out of the service says. She holds out a hand to Candace. "I'm Gloria. I took over the Chat and Chew from your mother." The Chat and Chew is a Wednesday-night church potluck that Laurel quit a few months ago, disgusted that a woman's devotional had devolved into little more than a gossip session. She told this to Candace over the phone during one of their awkward Thursday calls, claiming, "You put three women in a room together and forget it. They'd rather talk about shoes than God. Give them a reality show and they can yak about it for days, but ask them about Original Sin and you can hear the crickets chirp. Stupid women."

"Nice to meet you," Candace says and shakes Gloria's hand. Another boy sits next to Wally, no doll to comfort him, his hair fire red. His wrists are meaty and thick, more like a man's than a child's, and there's a scab on his arm that looks like a rug burn. He smiles at her in an uneasy way, all of his teeth exposed. "What happened exactly?"

"This is Todd," Gloria begins, and Laurel steps forward with her finger extended.

"This is trouble."

"There's been some trouble, yes," Gloria says, and Wally leans against his grandma, his arm around her waist.

"Let me guess," a man behind Candace says, and she turns and is confronted with Keith Danvers, her grade-school bully. He has the same red hair as the boy, the same meaty build, and as she glances at the kid again she's transported back to third grade, the same age Wally is now, and he is so clearly Keith's son that looking at him is like peering down a long tunnel into her past. Keith puts his hand on the boy's shoulder and squeezes. "You take a bite out of this kid?"

"That's exactly what happened," Gloria says, nodding her head, clearly glad to have the cards on the table. "We were studying Galatians 5, and he leaned over and bit this poor boy on the arm." Wally pulls up his sleeve and there are two semicircles on his flesh, a ghostly smile.

"Good Christ," Laurel says and turns on Keith. "You raising this animal?"

"Trying to," Keith says. "Kids have a mind of their own."

Laurel crosses her arms around Wally's chest, keeping her balance with the crutch. "Not if you're doing your job."

"This isn't the first incident," Gloria says meekly, and Keith moves his hand from his boy's shoulder to the back of his neck.

"I'll talk to him."

"You'd better," Laurel says.

"I'll gather the rest of your clan," Gloria tells Keith and disappears into the Sunday-school room.

He turns to Candace. "Candy Corin, nice to see you. You back visiting?"

"For a long weekend."

He nods toward Candace's mother. "Really long, I'm guessing."

Gloria emerges with three more redheads of varying sizes behind her. "All these are yours?" Candace asks, and Keith nods.

"Every one."

In the car on the way home, Laurel says, "You didn't do much to defend him," and Candace is stunned. She can't remember one incident from her childhood in which her mother defended her. That had been her father's job. Her mother's advice was to toughen up, to pull herself up by her bootstraps, that whatever was bothering her wasn't going to kill her. Laurel looks at her grandson in the rearview mirror. "You doing okay back there?" she asks Wally.

"Okey-dokey," he says to his grandma, and Laurel laughs.

"That's my boy," she says, and Candace stops herself from correcting her mother, from saying, "No, actually. He's mine."

When her father died a year ago, Candace and Jon had been separated for three months, and since that time she's gone back to nursing and started drinking two glasses of wine a night. She spent hours trolling dating websites and imagining the anger Jon would feel if she remarried first—how he would awake one morning in a shitty apartment with no one who loves him. Searching through the one-paragraph descriptions with spelling errors and ambiguous pictures (at best), she constructed a new husband around the absence of Jon, her rage converting to revenge. Her mother called one evening in January and told Candace her father was dead, from a heart attack that Laurel had watched from the kitchen window. "One minute he's driving the tractor down the lane to scoop snow, and the next it's heading toward the ditch and I'm thinking, 'what's that fool man up to now?'" Candace took the call in her own kitchen, her face reflected in the window like an apparition.

She hadn't told her family yet that she and Jon had separated, and the next day she called Jon at his new number, crying, and told him about her father and asked if he would go home with her. He said he would be happy to, that he wanted to be an ex-husband who would be there for her, an answer so self-serving it became in her mind's eye the reason they'd separated in the first place. As she stood near her mother—Wally between them, Jon on her other side—waiting for the pallbearers to bring her father's body and set it above the hole in the ground, her mother leaned over Wally and tucked a strand of hair behind Candace's ear. She turned toward her mother, her face melting into her mother's hand, and Laurel pursed her mouth. "You need a haircut," she said. After the funeral, Candace left Jon downstairs to fend for himself and ignored her mother's instructions to serve coffee to the guests. She and Wally lay down on the single bed of Candace's childhood, and she took

him point by point through the long-gone decor: the poster of
Michael Jackson in a pale-yellow sweater that had hovered above
her bed, an ad on the wall for Guess jeans with Anna Nicole leaned
over a convertible, a stuffed Opus on the nightstand—the room of
her childhood summoned before her.

In the house now there are signs everywhere of her father's
absence. His rifle collection is no longer in the mudroom attached
to the garage. The large radio where he listened to the farm reports
every day at the kitchen table is gone, replaced by a small TV. The
dining-room table is in the garage, the china hutch suspiciously
absent. "You get robbed?" Candace asked when she entered the
house after the thirteen-hour drive the night before, and Laurel
snorted. "Make it easier if I would," she said. "I don't know what
I'm going to do with all this stuff. That's just what it is too: stuff.
Who needs it?"

After church Laurel hands Wally the remote as he settles in a
nest on the floor, the carpet a vibrant maroon where Candace's
father's La-Z-Boy sat for two decades. "Knock yourself out," Laurel
tells Wally. "Fifty channels."

"That's it?"

"I got you some DVDs from the library too." She points to a stack
next to the TV, a large flat screen attached to the wall.

"That's a new TV," Candace says.

"The people on Fox News are the only ones I talk to all day, I
might as well be able to see them." Candace feels a flare of anger
at the subtext—"since my own daughter doesn't call me, only vis-
its once a year." She thumbs through the stack of DVDs, all action
flicks, some rated PG-13. At this age Candace wasn't allowed to
watch TV before 7:00 p.m. when evening programming started,
unless it was Wednesday and her mother had church group and
her father came in early from chores. Then they'd sit down at 6:30
and watch *Wheel of Fortune*, a show she still watches sometimes as
she's making dinner.

In the kitchen Laurel leans her crutch against the fireplace and switches on the small TV, the one that used to be in the living room, and lowers the volume to zero. She preheats the oven to three-fifty then limps to the fridge, declining Candace's offers of help. Laurel pulls out an egg casserole and orange juice. "You still take this?" she asks shaking the small carton of half-and-half at Candace, and Candace nods. The theme song for *iCarly* starts in the living room. "Amazing," Laurel says as she pours three glasses of juice. "It took me a week to figure out how to run that remote. I keep a cheat sheet tucked in the sofa cushions in case I get Alzheimer's."

"How will you remember where you put it?" Candace asks and Laurel laughs. Despite all the problems she has with her mother, they've always shared their sense of humor.

"Your father was scared to death of losing his mind. He used to do Sudoku puzzles every night. He memorized the state capitols out of a grade school textbook he bought at an estate sale a few years ago." Laurel leans her hip against the counter, the weight off her left leg. "He never would have guessed his body would go first."

"You doing okay?"

Laurel pushes off the counter and slides the casserole in the oven. "That woman you met, Gloria? She's not even a Lutheran. She came over from the Methodists a few years ago and is trying to take over the world."

"Starting with the Chat and Chew?"

Laurel pulls three placemats from a drawer, plates from the cupboard. "Good a place as any."

"Let me do that," Candace insists and sets the table as Laurel remains standing. "Did they kick you out?"

"We've been good members of that church all our lives," she says. "Don't get me started on the world going down the tubes."

Candace knows what most likely happened: her mother pissed someone off, got on her bossy high horse, and rode it all over town. She is about to push her mom on the truth but then realizes her mother still talks in the plural, that she has not fully conceived a life without her husband. She can't imagine her mother making her way through social situations without the earnestness of her father to soften the blow, the kind way he was able to diffuse her.

Candace reaches in the breadbox for the bag of sweet rolls she knows will be there, the same brand she ate after church every Sunday as a child, one of the few store-bought sweets her mother allowed in the house. She gathers the silverware from the drawer, and once it is arranged on the table, she and her mother sit down with their cups of coffee warming their hands in the drafty house. Candace knows without looking that the thermostat is set at sixty-six to keep the bills low, cardigans and afghans in every room.

"You have a doctor look at that ankle yet?" Candace asks, and Laurel shakes her head, blowing on the hot coffee. "Let me see," she says and reaches toward her mother, but Laurel scoots her leg under the table.

"What's done is done," she says. "I have enough sense to know it's just a sprain."

"Even so, that can be serious," Candace says, and her mother turns the volume up on the television. "Fine. Don't let me look at it. I'm only a trained nurse, you know. I only drove thirteen hours to try and help. Maybe later you and your stubbornness can go for a run."

"My stubbornness and your martyrdom. I wonder who would make it to the finish line first." Laurel takes another sip. "And don't get fresh with me."

Candace gets up and dumps the rest of her coffee in the sink. "I came here to help," she says.

"Then call your son for dinner. It's time to eat."

Candace and her mom make it two full days without a real fight. In those days Wally and his grandmother build a snowman, drive the tractor up and down the lane, and bake pecan sandies from scratch with Laurel's secret ingredient of coconut. She showed her grandson how to latchwork, and he started an owl wall-hanging kit for his bedroom in Park Ridge. They have filled their hours while Candace has lain on the couch ignoring her mother's requests to go through her father's things, Laurel insisting that Candace make some hard-headed decisions about what to keep and what to toss. She told her mom they would stay through Wednesday, but Monday after dinner Laurel drags all the mementos from the attic, insisting Candace go through them: the bicentennial pictures from 1976 when he grew a beard and Candace wore an old-fashioned Holly Hobby dress with a bonnet, and they walked side by side in the Pilgrim parade; her father's high school yearbooks; the coin collection he had since childhood; the ledgers he kept for the farm, his spidery script on every page. Candace doesn't want to go through the boxes. What she wants is to lie on the couch next to Wally and watch Bruce Willis blow things up. To think about her next boyfriend and how he will look like Bruce Willis. She and Bruce will be having dinner at Spiaggia when they run into Jon, who will be eating alone. Even better, he will be there in sweatpants getting takeout, a dish for one. She isn't sure if Spiaggia does takeout, but if not, maybe they can make an exception.

"I need you to look at this junk," Laurel says, hobbling into the living room with the first box, and when Candace doesn't answer Laurel starts for the front door. "Fine. I'll take it to the dump."

"Jesus," Candace says, following after her mother, grabbing her coat on the way, not wanting to subject Wally to any more bickering. He's heard enough between her and his own father the last few years. "What's the big hurry?"

"I'm moving. I'm selling the farm."

Candace is stunned although the evidence is everywhere. Yesterday she was looking for a pen for her crossword and opened drawer after empty drawer in her father's desk before finding a golf pencil in the kitchen. She shakes her head. "This is a rash decision. It's just because you fell."

Laurel hugs the box closer. "I fell two months ago."

"Jesus Christ, Mom. Why didn't you tell me?"

Laurel continues toward the pickup. "I bought a duplex in town, a one bedroom. I didn't want to bother you."

"You think it's a bother to tell me you're moving? It's not just your house. Maybe I want to live here," she says and instantly feels like her mother backed her into this statement, both of them aware how ridiculous it is.

"What're you going to do? Raise chickens?"

"You haven't had chickens in twenty years."

"See? Another dream down the tubes."

"You can't just throw his things away and forget about him," Candace says.

"Don't I know it." Her mother hands over the box with her father's collection of windup clocks. "What am I going to do with a box of clocks? I don't have anywhere to be."

"Fine," Candace says and puts it in the backseat of her Volvo. "I'll haul it to the dump right now."

"Good riddance," Laurel says and goes back in for Candace's collection of prom dresses, the box topped off with a pair of ice skates.

"We're leaving in the morning," Candace says to her mom as they load the hatchback. "I shouldn't be gone from work so long. I need to get Wally back to school."

"I thought you were staying until Wednesday." Laurel holds up her hand. "Save it," she says. "You do what you want, but don't lie to me about it." There is no winning. Candace gets behind the wheel and puts her key in the ignition. "You remember where the dump is?" her mom asks. "God knows you haven't been here much the last twenty years to refresh your memory."

"I think I can find it," Candace says.

There are two bars in town—the Standard and the OK Corral; the OK is where people in their twenties and thirties go before they graduate up to the Standard, accepting they're now townies and will never leave.

She takes a seat at the OK bar, the stool worn and soft. There is a sparse Monday crowd gathered in the back by the pool table and dartboards. Two women sit at the end of the bar in too-tight tank tops, giggling like they might be underage, their arms goose-pimpled against the cold.

"What can I get you?" the bartender asks. He's younger than Candace, she guesses by ten years, and he cocks his head to the side and squints an eye as he lights a cigarette. Cigarettes. She used to love those.

"You got a vending machine?" she asks, motioning to the cigarette.

"In the back." He pushes a button on the cash register and digs out a handful of quarters. "The dollar part's broke. They're six bucks."

"Six bucks?" she asks, incredulous. In college she and her girl-friend swore they'd quit smoking when cigarettes got up to two dollars a pack, and then again at three.

"You don't have to buy them," the bartender says, but he con-tinues counting the quarters in stacks.

Candace gathers the change and slides off her stool, stopping at the jukebox on her way back from the cigarette machine. She puts in four quarters and picks songs by Johnny Cash, Waylon Jennings, Garth Brooks. She doesn't listen to this music at home, but as the twangy beats make their way into the bar she wonders why not. It's uplifting to listen to other people's misery. Back on her stool she lights a cigarette and rests her elbows on the bar, listening to the happy sadness of the music, the clanging of the pool balls in the back. There's a squeal, and she turns to see the two girls from the end of the bar have joined the game, one leaning over the table to take a shot, her tank top riding up her slim back to show a smooth, tan swath of land. It is a long moment before Candace realizes she is staring and averts her gaze, in time to see that one of the men playing pool has been staring at her. Her heart jumps in her chest at the surprise of meeting someone's eyes. Keith Danvers.

He puts a hand in the air but doesn't move it, just short of a wave. He hands his pool cue to one of his buddies and makes his way to the bar and sits next to her, circling a finger at the bartender to indicate another round for him and her.

"You don't have to buy me a drink," she says.

"I know," he says and sets his palms on the bar.

"And if I drink it, it doesn't mean I've forgiven your kid." She peers up at him. "Your kid or you. You remember what a bully you were in school?" she asks, and Keith nods.

"I do. I was a bully a good chunk of my life, but I'm trying to change."

"You used to torture people when we were younger. Beating up kids smaller than you. Teasing the fat girls. When I got lice in fifth grade you called me a leper and made everyone else in class call me one too." Candace can still remember the nurse's hands flowing through her hair every year with great efficiency, creating parts, the rubber feel of the gloves against her scalp. And then, in fifth grade, the woman's hands stopped, and when they started moving again, they moved much more slowly. Keith was next in line and by the time Candace made it back to the classroom, where she had to wait for her mother in the hall while the teacher gathered her books, everyone knew. "I don't care if you're trying to change," she says to Keith. "That doesn't make it all right."

He looks at her, surprised. "I never said it did."

He turns toward the pool table and she puts a hand near his elbow. "Wait," she says. "Sorry." She holds up her beer can as thanks and lifts it to her mouth, realizing only when the metal touches her lips that the bartender didn't open it and she looks like a fool. She sets down the can, cracks the top, and tries again. Keith is drinking soda. "Thank you."

He points at the pack of cigarettes next to her purse. "A nasty habit."

"Here," she says and pushes the pack toward him.

He tilts his head to the side like the bartender and lights a cigarette, smoke winking his eye shut. "I'm sorry Todd bit your kid."

"Does he do that a lot?"

"More than you'd hope."

Candace draws the can of beer in a circle against the bar, leaving a trail of condensation. "What does his mother say about it?" She winces, knowing it sounds like a pickup line, like she is digging to see if he is single, but she isn't—at least she doesn't think she is. Although what a great story that would be to end up with her childhood bully after all these years, to get to tell everyone she meets she is with a man who knew her as a baby, although who would she tell? It would mean she is living in Pilgrim and everyone would already know their story. Besides, this is a town where almost everyone is married to someone they knew as a baby.

"She's been gone about two years," he says.

Candace looks up abruptly. "Oh. I'm sorry."

"Left us high and dry." He gives her what appears to be a genuine smile. "You remember that old Kenny Rogers song? 'You picked a fine time to leave me, Lucille'? It was like that. 'Four hungry kids and a crop in the field.' Just like that."

"I'm sorry," Candace repeats.

"Her name is even Lucille. Can you beat it? Although we called her Lucy. Or Luce."

"Lucy Twill? The other redhead in the class?"

He takes a sip of his soda through the thin straw, the ones people use to stir their drinks but normally don't drink from. "The one and only."

Candace grins. "Your high school sweetheart."

"Exactly. My high school sweetheart."

The song flips from Johnny Cash to Garth Brooks, his classic about friends in low places. "You don't drink," Candace says signaling Keith's soda as the bartender brings another round, this one on her.

"Nope," and Keith leaves it at that.

She takes a sip of her new beer, careful this time to make sure it's open. They sit for a while and listen to the clank of the pool balls, "Beast of Burden" by the Stones starting on the jukebox, Mick with a mouthful of longing.

"Your folks still out on the farm?" he asks, and she tells him her father died a year ago and he shakes his head. "I'm sorry, I knew that. What an asshole for forgetting." He tells a story about seeing her parents at the Standard a few years ago on New Year's Eve. They won a pitch tournament and as a prize, in addition to a Pepperidge Farm cheese basket, were brought on stage at midnight to kiss in front of the crowd. "Your old man bent your mom at the waist, leaned her back, and laid one on her. They could barely stop laughing long enough to kiss." It brings tears to Candace's eyes imagining this scene between her parents, this version of them she never knew. "I was there with Luce," Keith says. "I thought we were having the time of our lives, but she'd already put a security payment down on an apartment in Hartley."

Candace thinks of the missing furniture in the farmhouse, the empty drawers, the stack of four plates where there used to be eight. "I'm already drunk," she says as the bartender brings another set of drinks. "I shouldn't drink so fast."

Keith pulls another cigarette from her pack. "If you're too drunk to drive you might as well keep drinking." He puts the cigarette in her mouth and flicks the thumbwheel. "I have a truck out front and I'm sober as a stone. I'll be able to get you home."

Two hours later, Candace is straddling Keith in the driver's seat of his Dodge Ram, her knees buckled up near her armpits. *How is this done again?* He puts his cold hand under her shirt and slides it to the front, squeezing her breast through her padded bra so she barely feels it, Keith with a handful of fabric and foam. It's sweet really, she thinks, that he doesn't put his hand *under* the bra, which would make more sense, and they stay like this for what feels like a long time, a cramp starting in her left thigh, just kissing. She imagines her father coming out on the porch, one of his old shotguns in his hands, but then she remembers her mother cleared out the guns, followed by the memory that he is dead. What started out as a passionate lunge across the console has hit its peak, and Candace pushes off Keith's door and lands with an *oomph* in the passenger seat. She wonders if it was something Keith always wanted to do, kiss her back in high school, but listening to him talk about Lucy—his voice edged in bitterness—it is obvious he has loved his wife for a long time.

"I'm sorry about this," she says.

Keith laughs and pulls his shirt down over his belly—hairy while Jon's had been smooth—and Candace reaches into the footwell and pulls up her purse. "That's what a guy wants to hear after a make-out session in his truck. 'I'm sorry.' Me too then, I guess."

"That's what it was, huh? A make-out session?"

"Tried and true. You'll have a bruise tomorrow from the gear shift to prove it."

"Do high schoolers still do this? It's ridiculous."

"My oldest's sixteen, and yes, they do."

"She tells you?" She can't imagine telling such a thing to her father.

"Would it be better if she didn't?"

Candace shrugs. "Good point."

"I'm the guy whose daughter makes out in cars and whose son bites." He pulls a cigarette from a soft pack tucked in his visor. "The third one seems pretty normal, but who knows, it's early. Maybe she'll be the worst of them all."

"There's nothing wrong with your kids," Candace says.

"I'm kidding. I know." He lights the cigarette. "Best damn kids in the world. I love them like my own."

"Aren't they?"

"You need to loosen up, Candy. Take a joke."

Outside the pickup, the dark engulfs them. It doesn't get dark like this in Chicago, even in the suburbs, and the sweet smell of cold manure and the night sounds of the world make her wonder if she could have a life with Keith Danvers, stuck here in the country outside Pilgrim. Keith hands her his cigarette and she takes a drag, the beginning of a hangover making its way to the forefront.

She doesn't understand how her mother can pack up this house as if she is the only one who has ever lived here, make this kind of decision on her own. The house is full of memories. "When I had lice my mom had to burn the sheets. She cut off my hair and burned that too. The house smelled like burned hair for a week."

"I had crabs once," Keith offers.

Candace starts laughing and chokes on the smoke. "You shouldn't tell a woman something like that. You'll never get me to sleep with you now."

"You have your purse in your lap. I figured that ship had sailed."

"Was that why your wife left?"

"She was already gone by then. I was alone."

"Not one night, it sounds like."

"No, you're right," he says. "And then not for a month after that, not with my million little friends." She misses this, the intimacy, hearing secrets in the dark. The kitchen light comes on and she expects to see her mother's face through the window, but instead she sees Wally open the pantry and peer in.

"Listen," Keith starts. "I know I was a bully in grade school and junior high, high school even, but when I fell for Lucy I turned into a puddle. I wanted to apologize for every wrong I ever did. I wanted to say sorry to the ground for having to walk on it, I just didn't know how. I'm sorry," he says. "I really am."

They talk for a few more moments about the old times, then she kisses him on the cheek, opens the door, and jumps down from the truck, her feet unsteady on the gravel. "Thanks for a fun night," she says. "I'm sorry to hear you had crabs."

"It happens," he says. "What can you do?"

Inside, Wally closes the pantry quickly as his mother comes

through the door. "I'm hungry," he says. "I can't help it." Candace suffers a well of guilt that he feels bad about this, that he has been teased about his weight at school, that he has been picked on by other kids, and worst, that she has also berated him about it even though she has a sleeve of Thin Mints in her suitcase upstairs that she eats at night in the bathroom.

"Here," she says and leads him to the table. "I'll make you a snack. What're you in the mood for?"

He thinks for a moment. "A grilled cheese?"

She opens the fridge and locates the ingredients. "You got it." She pulls a skillet off the rack above the stove and puts in a generous pat of butter, holding the knob to the right as the gas lights. "What else?"

Clasped in his hand is Blanket Puppy, a stuffed animal his father bought him when he was two years old and that he only revisits in times of trouble. "Doritos?"

She opens the pantry. "How about sesame crackers?"

"That'll work."

She pulls out the bread and slathers two pieces with butter, placing thick pieces of cheese in between. She puts a bite of cheddar in her mouth and decides to make herself one too. Wally doesn't ask her where she's been or why she's just getting home, only sits at the table waiting for his sandwich. They eat them dunked in a pool of ketchup, their fingertips saturated with grease and crumbs. After they finish, she puts the dishes in the sink and the ketchup in the fridge, and when she asks Wally if he's ready for bed he asks if he can have another.

She pauses and he says to never mind, but she says, "No, no, it's fine. If you want another sandwich, I'm happy to make one for you."

She repeats the process, getting the ketchup back out and setting it on the table, slathering the bread with butter and pressing the cold cheese between the slices. She watches him as he eats this time. He stops after most bites and wipes his hands on his napkin, conscious of being watched. His hair, mussed from a few hours' sleep, sticks up in the back like a turkey's tail, just like it did when he was a baby. She reaches over and attempts to smooth it down, surprised when he doesn't flinch away.

"I'm done," he says and runs a finger across the plate and sticks it in his mouth.

"What else?" she says. "What can I fix you?" She wants at this moment to put the entire kitchen in front of him.

"I'm good," he says and yawns. He reaches for Blanket Puppy and she sees his stomach as his T-shirt pulls higher, the skin flabby and vulnerable. It's hard going through school with lice or a fat stomach. It's hard being a kid with a dad only on the weekends or an adult with no dad at all. His shirt drops back into place as he stands up, and Candace thinks of the girl at the bar—her thin, tan stomach peeking out from under her tank top—but she thinks of it merely because they are both stomachs, then pushes the thought away and steers Wally to their room.

The next morning Candace insists on taking her mother and Wally to the Standard for breakfast, a last-ditch effort to end on a peaceful note. "Where's your car?" Laurel asks as they come out of the house, the crutch secured in her armpit. Her mother is stiffest in the morning but can usually manage without the crutch through the second half of the day. Candace remembers her car, parked next to Keith's truck when she stumbled out of the OK, her father's life in the backseat. "Never mind," Laurel said. "I can bring you to it after breakfast."

Todd, Keith's youngest, is sitting at the restaurant counter next to two old video game machines. Candace scans the restaurant quickly while smoothing her hair, but the only other redhead she sees is a skinny girl on a stool in too-tight jeans, the crack of her butt displayed. Candace shuffles her mother and Wally toward the back room hidden behind the corner where there is a stage by the north wall for cover bands on the weekend, where Candace's father bent her mother at the waist for a kiss. They peruse the menus in silence. Wally asks his mother if it's okay if he gets the pancakes and bacon, and she nudges him toward oatmeal and a juice. After the waitress takes their orders, Wally begs to go up front to play Street Fighter Two, and Laurel digs in her purse for a few quarters, handing them over along with a dollar bill, saying he can get change at the hostess stand.

Candace is glad now that she ate a sandwich the night before, her hangover more like a memory. "So where's the house?"

"On Vandalia Street. Next to Rip Walsh's old place."

Candace nods. She hasn't lived in this town for almost twenty years, yet she can picture the street, Rip Walsh out in black socks and sandals raking his yard.

"You like it, then?"

Laurel scrubs at an invisible spot on the Formica tabletop. "It's fine. The appliances are older than the hills, but it's not like I'm going to live there forever. Or if I do, forever won't be that long."

Candace feels a tightening in her chest. She was shocked when her father died, even though throughout her childhood his immortality was constantly questioned. When she was eight he cut his neck with a machete while walking beans; her thirteenth birthday he lost a finger to a thresher; when Candace was in high school he developed a blood infection from a hog bite. After she left home she worried less and less about her father, the accidents growing less frequent, but she realizes now that it was only because her parents stopped calling with the news. "Is there something you're not telling me, something else?" She pauses, her stomach bottoming out. "Are you sick or something?"

Laurel snorts. "I'm not sick, I'm just old."

The waitress sets their coffees down, and Candace reaches for an individual creamer, shaking it in her hand before pulling back the tab. "You remember when I had lice?"

Her mother clutches a hand dramatically to her chest. "Do I? You cried for a week straight. You were allergic to the shampoo so we had to get a doctor's brand, and you cried the whole way to the drugstore and back. You were so embarrassed that the pharmacist would know. He had a kid a grade above you."

"I remember that," Candace says. "Dad took me to the Dairy Freeze afterward and bought me a sundae. I ate it in the car, even though I wasn't supposed to."

"I remember," Laurel says, and Candace looks at her. "I know all kinds of things you thought were a secret."

"Like what?"

Laurel puts her elbow on the table, her chin in her palm. "Well, let's see. That you went to that rock concert in Omaha with Sheryl Collins when you were a sophomore. That your father caught you smoking cigarettes when you were fourteen with Nicole Doyle. That you were out last night with Keith Danvers."

Candace laughs. "You know about that?"

"I might have been kicked out of the Chat and Chew, but I still have my contacts." Laurel takes a sip of coffee.

"Has it sold yet?" Candace asks about the farm.

"Not yet, but it's listed with Ed Jackson. He sold your dad every tractor he ever drove. Started a real-estate business a few years ago."

"You don't need to sell the farm," Candace says.

"I don't have to keep it either."

The waitress comes and tells them their food will be up in a few seconds, and Laurel nods to the other room where Wally's hidden away with his video games. "How's he doing?"

Candace isn't sure if she means in the other room or since the divorce or with his grandfather in the ground. "Fine, I guess."

"You guess? He's your child. You should be doing better than guessing."

"How am *I* doing then?" Candace challenges her mother.

Laurel pats her daughter's hand one time. "Just fine," she says, and the answer, in its optimism, brings tears to Candace's eyes. What a shitty year it's been—her dad dying, the divorce—but not only for her. As she turns her chair toward her mother, Wally comes around the corner with Keith's son Todd and she sees a red smear around Todd's mouth. She feels the room slide to the left, sure it is blood, that Todd has again bitten her son. Only Wally is smiling, which doesn't make sense.

"Todd's sister bought us doughnuts," Wally explains, and holds up the Cherry Bismarck in his hand as he slides into his chair, powdered sugar on his chin so he looks as if he were blowing bubbles in the snow. "We're friends again."

Just like that, they are friends again. All their past sins forgotten.

Candace motions to the empty seat next to her. "Todd? You want to join us?"

"That's okay," he says and licks his fingers one by one, moving methodically down the line. "My sister's done flirting with the cook. We got to get to school." He turns to Wally. "Maybe next time you're in town you can come out to my house. I've got an Xbox 360."

"That'd be cool," Wally says and shrugs, a barely contained grin on his face. When Todd gets outside he knocks on the plate glass window and waves, his sister already at the car, a girl intent on walking three steps ahead of him. He leans in and kisses the window so boldly that Candace thinks she can hear it, than he pulls back and grins, pointing at the smeared red mouth left on the glass, his breath visible in the cold. Wally laughs and waves back, then turns and smiles at his mom. "He's cool," Wally says and Candace shakes her head.

"Someone's going to have to wash that window."

"Most likely a woman," Laurel adds.

The waitress sets their plates down along with their check and tells them to take their time. Laurel reaches for it before her daughter can, and Candace knows better than to argue with her mother. She imagines her mom out on the farm each night watching Bill O'Reilly or Shep Smith, yelling at her large, new television. "We'll be back in a few months," she says. "Help you get settled in your new place."

"Don't be silly. Gas prices as high as they are, you should wait at least six months."

"Maybe we'll fly."

Laurel snorts. "Into where? Omaha? You'd still have three hours to drive."

Candace wets the tip of her napkin in her water glass and hones in on Wally's face, the smear of powdered sugar. "Mom," he whines but she ignores him, pulling his cheek to the side as she tackles the spot.

"Oh," she says. "It's not going to kill you." And when she's done she puts both hands on his cheeks, pulls his head toward her mouth, and kisses the part in his hair.

The Good Neighbor

I was mowing on a Sunday late in the day when my neighbor Mary stumbled from her front door and crossed her yard into mine. She began speaking over the loud grind of the mower, her hands moving harshly through the air. I let the handle go and the mower died, her voice still loud in the now still evening. The sun was so intense my entire body was sweating and small shards of grass clung to my ankles and calves. I couldn't understand what she was saying, the words garbled next to other words that made no sense together. Her voice was thick with tears and her normally neat hair looked jagged at the ends, as if it had been cut with a dull, wet razor. She was wearing a white parka, an inappropriately warm coat for the hot day.

"Mary," I said. "What is it? What's happened?"

Mary spoke through the tears, nearly incomprehensible. It was something about her grandson, Josh, and an accident. I gathered he was in his car and hit another man. "He's dead," Mary said, and after more hysterics I figured out that the man was dead, not Josh. Josh was down at County Memorial having glass picked from his face, and could I bring her there? She had her car keys in her hand. "I don't trust myself to drive," she said.

"Of course. I'm happy to help." We stood staring at each other for a long moment—a surprisingly friendly look, as if we were just meeting and curious about the other. I left the mower on the half-cut lawn and ran inside to leave my wife a note saying I was taking Mary to the hospital. I looked at the note then wrote on the bottom *Josh was in an accident*, then, *He's okay.*

I opened the passenger door of my car and Mary climbed in, her hands twitching in her lap, flipping her keys over and over in a rhythm. I drove slowly. Josh had come to live with her six months ago after his parents moved to Pennsylvania for his father's job. What reason did Mary have to say no? A too-big house, plenty of money? Josh wanted to stay in Sioux Falls and finish out his junior year with his friends, but it was now July and he was still here. I was his algebra teacher and saw two sides to Josh: the mild boy he was with his grandmother, and the boy who skulked the halls at Lincoln High. And now this.

I drove to the front entrance and Mary scurried from the car, her parka catching on the door as she slammed it. She wrenched the coat back, ripping the tough nylon.

Inside, the emergency room was nearly empty. Two women in their twenties sat on hard plastic chairs, one with a young girl on her lap. The girl looked no more than seven, her legs in tiny jeans with a pink-and-purple butterfly sewn on the knee, at least twenty bright plastic barrettes in her hair. I wondered what they were here for. It was like seeing civilians in a police station: everyone looked guilty, or like they were associated with someone who was. Why did I assume it was something they were guilty of, rather than the body rebelling against itself? Kidney stones, laryngitis. It could have been anything. The stouter woman, the one without the child on her lap, looked at me, her mouth curling up. She looked like she wanted a cigarette and did not like me.

I approached the nurse's station where Mary was filling out paperwork for Josh. "I don't know the answers to these questions," she said, panic in her voice. "I don't know anything at all."

I took the paper from her. "What don't you know?"

"All of it. What kind of silly question is this?" She pointed randomly to the paper.

"Blood type."

"What grandmother would know that? We expect the best from our grandkids." She had left her purse at home and didn't have her insurance card. "He's already back there. What are they going to do? Not treat him? I'd like to see them try." It sounded like a threat.

I wondered where the body was, the man who had been killed. I looked around, although certainly they wouldn't leave it there in the lobby.

"When can I see him?" Mary asked the nurse.

"You need to stay calm, ma'am," the nurse stated. Her voice was reasonable, used to putting others in their place. Every word was meant to head off a possible confrontation, but you could tell if it veered in that direction the woman could handle it. "We'll let you back soon enough." It was the vagueness of the timeline—*soon enough*—that let me know we'd be there a while.

I led Mary to the row of chairs where the women were sitting. "I don't understand what could have happened," she said. "Why would Josh do something like this?"

"It wasn't on purpose."

She looked at me, surprised. "I know that! Where did you hear that?"

"I didn't, I'm sorry. I'm trying to reassure you." I put an awkward hand on her shoulder. "Would you like me to get you some coffee?"

"It's almost five o'clock. I can't drink caffeine after three."

So far, my interactions with Josh had been limited and he seemed for the most part like a good kid. Since he had come to live with his grandmother he'd taken over caring for her yard, what little space there was and what small amount of care it required. But he was lazy, a teenager, and had taken to dumping the clippings over the fence and into my yard. At night I gathered them as well as my own and dumped them back, the pile growing with each flip over the fence. Now my tomatoes were dying and I wondered why. Word had gotten out at school that he was living next to me, and his friends—other average teenage boys—would come over in the evening and howl like wolves, throw small rocks at my windows, tip over my garbage cans. I'm neither a disliked teacher nor a particularly well-liked one either. I'm fair. I ride that middle ground teenagers distrust so much, every emotion an extreme. When his friends weren't around, Josh would smile halfway and say, "Hey, Mr. Dalton," but when his friends were there he'd not so much as nod. One time I turned around quickly to find him in front of his pack, his right arm righteously extended as he flipped me off, but I could tell from the splotches on his cheeks he felt silly and wrong doing it. Now he had killed someone and he was seventeen and no matter what he did for the rest of his life, nothing would erase that. When I was in high school my friends and I tried to get dates with popular girls with long, pretty hair and thin hips. When that failed, we made out with fat girls that we never called and ignored the next Monday in the halls. It's nothing I'm proud of now, that we enabled those girls to feel worse about themselves. My wife told me without self-consciousness that in high school she was thin, beautiful, and well liked. I thought these pasts, even though we didn't know each other back then, created a rift between us, a power differentiation in our relationship that was evident today.

I told Mary I would get her something to drink and set off in search of a vending machine or cafeteria. In the basement—the worst possible place to serve food, with fluorescent lights and damp air—I found a small industrial café and ordered us two cups, forgetting until it was too late to get Mary decaf. One of the women from upstairs was down there now, the one without the child. I nodded and smiled and she looked at me, her eyes squinting shut.

"I'm sorry," I said instinctually.

She continued squinting, her nose getting in on the business. "I lost my glasses. I can't see anything. I wondered if you were Theresa."

"Is that the woman you were with upstairs?"

"Yes."

"I'm not her."

The woman laughed. "Why you have to ask who she was before you said you weren't her? Were you thinking maybe you were?"

I shrugged before remembering she couldn't see me. "Maybe."

Back upstairs Mary was gone from the waiting room. I sat with the two cups of coffee balanced on my knees. It felt good, like it had been a long time since I had the balance of two cups of coffee. I knew I had to call my wife and explain the note.

Mary came back, her face awash in a new round of tears. "I saw him. He's in the back, lying down. It looks like he's taking a nap." I was unsure whether or not she was talking about Josh or the man he had killed and decided to let her keep going until this issue became clear. It did in time, and I realized she was talking about her grandson.

"I need you to talk to him. He needs a father figure right now."

"I'm not qualified for that." Janey and I had never had children, although there was a time ten or twelve years ago when we talked about it. That lasted a few years and then it stopped.

"Then what are you doing here?"

"You needed a ride."

She looked at me, clearly exasperated. "I have a car."

I followed her back through the ER, to a gurney behind a curtain on a curved iron bar. She shuffled it back with a ringing of metal on metal and Josh's eyes fluttered open. He had small butterfly bandages on his face and a larger patch on his shoulder from the glass of the windshield. He was shirtless and his chest was tan and sunken, young looking, his right arm in a sling. From a log-like bump under the blanket I surmised his leg was in a cast of some kind.

"Mr. Dalton?" He looked at his grandmother. "Am I going to be expelled?"

"Of course not," I said. My chest contracted at the thought that expulsion was the punishment that had him most concerned. "Has your grandmother told you what happened?"

"The accident? I was there."

"I know. But do you know what happened?"

"I killed someone?" He answered as he would in school, in a tentative, questioning voice.

"That's right," I said. "Good. That's the correct answer."

Josh turned to me, a small bruise under both eyes. "I'm sorry about the grass."

He was referring to our lawn war, and I could tell from his apology he was trying to make amends where he could. "It's fine," I said. "Don't worry about that now."

Mary gripped my arm, her eyes intent on her grandson. "Tell him what this all means." I didn't know what she was referring to, but I could tell she was looking for a very specific answer, that this was a test I was failing.

"The man is dead," I said and Mary nodded.

"It's not your fault, Josh," she said and brought her hand from my arm to Josh's chest. "Not one bit of it."

"But I was driving."

"No," she said, more vehemently this time. "No. No."

Josh turned to me, his eyes questioning. "But I killed him?"

"That's true." I smiled ruefully. "I wasn't in the car. I don't know whose fault it was. Did the man run out in front of you?"

Mary left the room abruptly, the curtain quivering in her wake. I could hear her footsteps for a moment in the busy hall before they were swallowed up by other sounds.

Josh began to shake his head and winced, bringing his hand to his neck. "I didn't mean for this to happen. I thought I was paying attention." He looked at me, his eyes naked. "Have you ever done anything *really* bad?"

Of course I had, but where to start? I hadn't killed anyone. What came to mind was the opposite: the unwanted pregnancy of a girl I had dated in college. She decided to keep the baby and we concluded that I wouldn't be involved. The baby would be twenty-three or twenty-four by now. I didn't even know the sex of the child that was no longer a child. The mother, Susan Smith, said it was better this way. How would I ever locate a Smith this many years in the future? It's the name one pretends to have when she doesn't want to be found. "We've all done bad things. You can't let those decisions rule your life."

"I didn't *decide* to kill somebody!"

"We can't be accountable for every little thing."

"They're going to throw me in jail." His eyes widened. "I'm only seventeen and I'm going to get butt raped."

Josh's expression was earnest, a boy who feared many things. "Don't worry, son. They can't put you in jail if you're a minor." I had no idea if this were true but it seemed so from the cop shows I watched at night with Janey. I hadn't thought about that baby for a long time and would now often go stretches of not thinking about him or her. Stretches that would snap shut when the thought of my own mortality loomed in front of me and I'd know somewhere out there was a fragment of myself reading *War and Peace*, which I never got around to, or finally taking guitar lessons.

I put a hand on the smooth corner at the foot of Josh's bed. "You're going to be fine. In a few years it'll be like this never even happened."

"You're saying I'm just going to forget this?" I nodded. He looked relieved and horrified.

Mary came back in the room looking calmer. I wondered if she'd raided a prescriptions closet in the meantime, her lips firm and her eyes dry. "You need to go away," she said to me, her parka slung across her folded elbow looking damp and depleted.

"How will you get home?"

"Don't *abandon* me," she said, exasperated by my stupidity. "Just wait in the lobby."

I shuffled out from behind the curtain and back to the waiting room, which was filling up with other people, a late-night push.

The women were still there, eating chocolate cake the one with bad eyesight must have purchased in the cafeteria. The pieces were huge and I liked that. It was sad enough these people were eating cake in a hospital, they might as well get a lot of it. The nearsighted woman held out a piece of paper to me as I sat down next to her. "Does that look right to you?" I took the paper from her, unsure what I was looking for. It was an insurance statement. The young girl sat on the semi-clean floor with chocolate frosting on her lips that looked like it had been applied on purpose.

"Which part?"

She let out a stream of air and poked her finger at the paper. "They say my sister has to pay three hundred dollars just to be here. Can that be right?"

"I guess so."

"'Cause I don't have that kind of cash. I got the kind that jingles." She pulled on a thread at the bottom of her neon green shirt and it puckered the hem before releasing. I peered closer at the form, curious to know what her sister had and anxious to help, to prove my worth, as if this paperwork were another test. It reminded me of a TV show I saw once where people in a fancy gallery were asked to discuss the artistic merit of a dozen paintings. It was on PBS or maybe *60 Minutes*; it seemed like the kind of mean-spirited business you'd find on a network show. The critics and gallery attendees went on about the abstractness, the length of the brush stroke, the depth of the paint. Afterward they were told children had done the paintings—three- and four-year-olds at a nearby preschool— and *now* what did they think that said about art? It was an awful program, awful. All those people put in their place. I would have thought I'd feel victorious watching those snooty types get a cup of what-for, but it made me feel bad for them, embarrassed. Since then—and probably before then, although I hadn't realized it—I had worried that somehow, someone was playing a similar trick on me, calling me out as a fake. The child on the floor dipped a delicate finger in the cake and did indeed put the frosting on her lips, smearing it on like lip gloss. "I'm sorry," I told the woman, who had introduced herself as Charlene. "I'm no help at all."

Charlene pulled the sheet away and folded it in a square. "I don't know why I'm carrying insurance if they're going to pull this shit. If it costs this much to stay healthy maybe they just want us sick."

"I'm here for my neighbor," I volunteered. "He killed a man. With his car. It was an accident."

"For real?" She turned toward me, her mouth slack. "I knew a man one time got hit by a car so hard it nearly knocked some sense in him. It was a friendly tap on the gas. Tap tap." She tapped a fingernail against my thigh. "Tap."

"You hit him?"

She tapped her finger a second time before moving it back to her own lap. "Sometimes you got to learn a lesson the hard way to really learn it."

"Marvin Minsky says you have to learn things two ways before you really understand it." He was a mathematician who attempted to give common sense to robots, as if we had enough to go around.

"That's the truth. Gerry had to learn it through his ears and then through the back of his knees." She sniffed and looked up as an elderly man shuffled in and took the seat closest to the door. "Sounds like the man your friend killed only got the chance to learn it once, but I bet he learned it good." The old man looked at us suspiciously, as if he couldn't quite hear the words but knew we were up to no good.

I remembered Susan coming into my dorm room, the Pink Floyd poster on the wall, the stack of bowls covered in an orange crust of old mac and cheese. She hadn't known how to tell me—to pose this as a good thing or a bad thing. Her face was a mix of hopeful exuberance and dread. My reaction had been the same. We were both playing a role, trying to figure out what it was we were doing being adults. It was weeks later when I came to her apartment and told her I wasn't ready to be a father, as if the decision were really up to me. She looked at me liked she hated me and like she wished she could make a similar pronouncement. We spoke a few times after that—a slow break up, nothing as dramatic as a slammed door—but by the time the baby was born I was home in Yankton with my parents for the summer, and by the time I got back in fall she was in Illinois with her parents for good. She sent a baby picture to my folks' house—gender indiscriminant, wrapped in a yellow blanket—and I told them it was the child of a girl I knew at school, that we'd been in a stats class together, which was true. "Babies having babies," my mother said shaking her head and, putting a magnet shaped like a jelly jar against it, she snapped the picture to the fridge. Even a baby of a baby and a stranger deserved to be displayed on the fridge.

"I can't help you with the form, I'm sorry," I said, although Charlene had already put the form away. "I don't understand insurance policies."

"Me neither," she said, crossing her arms and slumping in the seat. "I don't know what I think I'm insuring against."

"What's wrong with your sister?"

Charlene looked at me sharply. "Not a damn thing. What's wrong with you?"

"I told you, my neighbor was in a car accident. I'm here with his grandmother."

"I'm here because my sister likes to date the wrong kind of men, and I keep swooping in to try and save her."

"Maybe she can't be saved."

She took the insurance policy out of her pocket and waved it around. "Then what's this for? That's what I keep wondering."

Josh's grandmother came around the corner with a determined look on her face. I saw that look often on the faces of my colleagues at the beginning of the school year, when we still hoped a little encouragement might be all the kids needed to reach their potential. Potential: such an elusive and fatigable thing. We taught arithmetic, reading skills, world history. It doesn't leave a lot of room for anything else in an eight-hour day, like what to do when you've killed a man. "He's going to be fine," Mary said and settled herself next to me, sliding back into the hollow of the plastic seat without meaning to. "I'm going to hire a lawyer to help with the specifics. This will all be cleared up tomorrow."

"I'm glad to hear it," I said.

Mary turned to me, the chair letting out a funny squeak like a fart and I had to rearrange my face to keep from laughing. Charlene eyed me suspiciously, shaking her head. "I don't understand how I'm supposed to call my daughter," Mary said, "and tell her what happened. I raised three children from infancy to adulthood and nothing bad happened. Now I've had my grandson six months and a man is dead." She sighed dramatically. "I taught my daughter everything there is to know about being a mother, and she's going to see this as my fault."

"It's nobody's fault."

She laughed, an uncomplicated sound. "How can you say that with a straight face?"

I had no idea.

We spent a few more hours in the waiting room—Mary writing scripts of what she'd say to the attorney and her daughter, so much coffee coursing through her system her hands began to pulse. Thereon and Charlene left with the child, saying they'd be back in the morning when they could visit their sister, dumb girl that she was.

I called Janey around midnight from a payphone a floor up, not wanting Mary to hear me. "Jesus, I've been worried sick." Janey had a throaty voice, full of emotion even when she was speaking in a monotone. I could hear the faint sound of rushing water behind her and knew she must be in the kitchen, her hip against the dishwasher. "You need to get a cell phone."

"I don't want a cell phone." My common complaint was that we lived in a world where people had forgotten to look up, their eyes always trained down on electronics. I'd look out at the start of each class period and see nothing but the crowns of heads as the children texted the person next to them. Besides, we had no children. Who would teach me how to use it?

"What time you think you'll be home?" she asked and I told her I hoped in the next few hours, that I wouldn't still be here in the morning, curious as I was to hear the reunion between the sisters. "You're a good neighbor to do this," Janey said and I stayed silent. "I mean it. You could have just dropped her at the door and come home."

"It's a good thing I didn't know that earlier."

"Phooey," she said. "You would have stayed." Janey knew about the baby and married me anyway. She was a firm believer in putting past mistakes behind you, this from a girl who had been pretty in high school. We stayed on the phone a few more minutes, mostly in silence listening to the sound of the other breathing. The dishwasher churned into another cycle and I hung up, my hand lingering on the warm receiver as I stared at the fingerprints littering the metal face of the phone. I thought about calling Susan but of course didn't have her number. Maybe I could find her on the Internet or hire a private investigator and show up at her house, a bundle of roses in one arm and a gift for the baby in the other—a stack of receiving blankets or those one-piece sleepers babies wear—but I was twenty-some years too late. The baby was gone. For all I knew, dead. There were some things you could spend a lifetime hoping to reverse, partly because you know you can't. If I could go back and do it again, I'd make the same regrettable decision. Better to live with regret than real consequences.

Mary and I left just after two o'clock, when Josh was settled in a room and it became apparent there would be no changes in his condition. Visiting hours would resume at eight a.m.

In the car, I could see from approaching headlights that Mary's eyes were ringed with dark circles that matched Josh's bruises, her face hollow as a skeleton's. I parked in her driveway and told her to get some sleep, that I'd be back over at a quarter to eight to take her to the hospital. Exiting her porch, I heard a trash can clatter onto the cement a street or two over. I could smell dirt and the faint, sickly sweet scent of the garbage cans lining the street for morning pick up. A dog howled a long, painful moan that turned into quick, deep barks, his voice catching at the end of each snap like he was eating his breath. I'd wished at my worst moments for the baby Susan and I had to miscarry, to take that complication out of my life.

I went into the bedroom. Janey was sleeping on top of the quilt, her breath labored in the thick summer. Josh would come home in a few days and restart his life, this one moment in time—the *tap tap tap* as Charlene had said—telling him more than he wanted to know about people, life, and death. Outside the lawnmower still sat in the middle of the yard, a line of short grass behind it then a line of long in front, and it seemed so simple to push that machine across the yard and have it all be the same, smooth, symmetrical. I pulled the starter cord on the mower and the engine sputtered once then caught, a noise so loud it seemed to eat the night, to consume the peace around me. I pushed forward, the grass disappearing and leaving a wake of newness behind me, the smell of fresh, wet grass awakening my senses. I turned at the corner and faced the house as the door flew open. Janey stood with her hands on her hips, her ticked-off stance of one foot jutted forward.

"It's two in the morning!" she said. I didn't even know what time the baby had been born. I cupped a hand to my ear and in return she cupped her hands to her mouth like a megaphone. "Two in the morning!"

"I'm just going to finish this," I said, pointing at the lawn, knowing she couldn't hear me. She stormed back inside, an angry woman with a fool for a husband.

I pushed through the row and turned again taking another swipe. When I finished I'd dump the clippings in Mary's yard, under Josh's window. It would be something to irritate him when he got back home, a return to his normal life. I imagined him out there in the humid July heat, sweat running in rivulets down his thin boy's chest as he tried to maneuver an arm in a sling, crutches in his armpits. He would have to find a new way of working his body in unison with the injuries, bending carefully to pick up a handful of dead grass. He would fling it over our shared fence and into my yard where I'd be waiting, full of remorse, to give the offering back again.

Dog People

Margie settles on the bench, her ankle hooked at the wheel of the stroller, rocking it back and forth. Movement is the only thing that stops the baby from crying, so this morning Margie spent fifteen minutes loading everything she might need into the stroller basket—diapers, wipes, an extra onesie, a bottle, blankets, hand sanitizer, a magazine she'll never read, her keys—all for a ten-minute walk to the park four blocks from their house, their first official outing that doesn't involve a doctor's visit. Katherine is three weeks old, but it's hard to think of her as Katherine and not the baby. Who at three weeks old has enough personality to fit a name? Margie hopes when the baby grows up the name will suit her. If not, there's always Katie or Kate or Kit Kat. She'd like to have a spark plug named Kit Kat, but chances are she'll be a Katherine (Margie realizes she's actually a Margaret). At home, at night, Katherine screams for hours on end, but here in the park she is quiet. The baby, even at three weeks, seems to follow Margie with her eyes, like one of the black-cat clocks with the swinging tail whose large plastic eyes survey the room back and forth.

A man in a black rubber apron and work boots comes over and sits next to Margie on the bench and lights a cigarette. It's mid-September and the weather has just started to turn from mild summer to the beginning of fall, a slight breeze blowing through the hair on Margie's perpetually sweaty neck.

"I'm sorry," she says and stands to leave but then sits back down. Why should she be the one to leave if he's smoking? The smell is neither pleasant nor unpleasant, but she knows it's bad for the baby. She hates confrontation and would rather get up herself than ask him to leave. But the baby is quiet, and Margie's own body so tired. She settles back on the bench. She hasn't slept through the night since her seventh month of pregnancy. She assumed once she didn't have this baby kicking around inside her, along with the worry of how the delivery would go, she'd finally be able to sleep. How shortsighted that was. How ridiculously wrong. The apron the man is wearing is covered in small white hairs, and Margie instantly thinks of pubic hairs, which causes her crotch to itch. There is so much about giving birth she hadn't anticipated. Of course, in hindsight, how could she not realize they would shave part of her pubic area, that she might shit on the bed when she was pushing for hours on end?

The man gestures to his apron. "It's a poodle," he says.

"Excuse me?" Margie says. To the left is an aluminum slide and four swings, a teeter-totter that looks like a dinosaur. She has never been to this park before, even though it is only four blocks from her house. She imagines the hours and summers they'll log here in years to come—how much fun it will be to teach Kit Kat to swing—but now there is nothing they can do. She pushes the stroller with her ankle, then pulls it back.

"The hair. It's from a poodle. I work at Trudy's." He gestures across the street with the hand holding the cigarette, and she sees Trudy's Salon and Boarding, a building she's never noticed before, the letters on the sign a garish neon pink.

She looks at her baby, embarrassed suddenly by the baldness of Katherine's head. "Sounds like a fun job."

The man shrugs. Margie guesses him to be in his midthirties, with a scruffy beard of three to four days, a smudge of dirt or grease on his damp pants. He is what she would call unconventionally attractive if anyone would think to ask her, a category she knows she's nowhere near with her tummy like rising dough, her hair unwashed for as many days since this man last shaved; if anything, she is conventionally unattractive. "Not really," he says and takes a drag on the cigarette. "But I love dogs, even ones with stupid haircuts." He holds out his free hand. "I'm Jim."

Margie stares at it for a moment before taking it in her own, the dryness of his hands mirroring her own now that she washes them fifty times a day. "I'm Margie," she says and motions to the stroller. "This is Kit Kat."

"Cute kid."

"You think so?" She looks at the baby. Katherine has large blue eyes, so dark the pupils seem to eat the irises; her nose looks like it was sculpted from clay. She wonders if the baby is really beautiful. She thinks so, but other times, not.

"She's a looker." He takes another drag off his cigarette as Margie watches the kids in the sandbox—two young boys in matching khaki jackets. She is glad she had a girl, that the baby will be able to wear things other than khaki and blue, that she won't have to dress her child like a middle-aged office drone. The man clears his throat and spits to the side, and it's as if Margie has come to into a moment of silence. She wonders if he asked a question and if it is still there between them, if she was supposed to answer.

"Do you have kids?"

"Two, a boy and a girl. Neither one was as cute as yours though." Katherine coos like a pigeon, her large dark eyes watching her mother. What does she see? According to the books, nothing— everything is hazy—but Margie doesn't think so, feeling constantly judged by the tiny eyes.

"What's it like, grooming dogs?" Margie asks.

He takes another drag off the cigarette, holding the smoke in long enough that Margie wonders if he hasn't recently given up the habit only to fail and start again. "It's what you'd suspect. You like some dogs better than others, but even the ones you don't like are better than most people." He looks at Margie, her foot coming to rest on the stroller. "You a cat person?"

"I like dogs."

He looks at her from under the thin trail of smoke. "I'd bet money you were a cat person."

Margie can tell this is not a compliment, that he values cats about as much as he does people. "How old are your kids now?"

"Six and eight. The girl's a handful. She's into eye makeup. Wears that shit all over town." He pauses a moment. "Wait. She's nine. Had a birthday about a month ago."

"I can't imagine this baby will ever be nine." Three weeks ago she'd never guessed the baby would make it to three weeks. When they pulled the baby from the pocket of Margie's body and held her in the air, Margie felt such emptiness and fullness she didn't know how she could contain such a contradiction without bursting apart.

"Why you say that? Is she sick?"

"No," Margie says, alarmed at the idea. "Of course not." She glances at her watch, than stands to leave. It's almost six, which means Leo will be coming home from work soon, which means there will be someone else to watch the baby. Margie will be able to stand in her kitchen all by herself and open a can with a can opener, or open the fridge and just stare inside. These are her moments alone now, what it means to be an independent woman.

"She's a good-looking baby," the man says again. "She looks just like you."

Margie pauses from tucking the blanket around Katherine, so flustered by the comment. It strikes her as vaguely inappropriate—she's the mother of a three-week-old baby!—as well as inaccurate, but it is also unreasonably flattering. "Good luck with the dogs."

He nods at the stroller. "Good luck with the baby."

"I need it," she says, than laughs to show it's all a joke, that clearly she has motherhood under control. Margie bumps the stroller over the grass and makes her way to the sidewalk, stopping to wave good-bye. Jim lifts his cigarette in the air in a jaunty salute before throwing it on the ground and crushing it with his foot.

She turns left to travel the four blocks back to her house. She imagines Leo on his way home, Wilco blaring through the speakers of the Honda, his personal pod of independence. When he gets home he'll slip Kit Kat in the crook of his arm and she'll fall instantly asleep while he plays *Call of Duty: Black Ops* on the PlayStation 3. Somehow, Leo has managed to retain his old life, to fit Kit Kat into his world as neatly as she fits in his arm, while Margie will hide in the kitchen, holding her breath, the pantry full of canned goods offering no answers.

Margie takes to walking in the park every day around five o'clock. After the first trip, Katherine slept for forty-five minutes in a row. She tells Leo and her mother on the phone that the walks are good for Katherine, that Katherine loves to be outside, that she is an Outside Baby. It is an anecdote Margie can pull out like a shiny present to show everyone that she is a Mother who understands her Daughter, that there is something that differentiates Katherine from other babies.

Some days Margie has to wake Katherine from her nap and set her howling so she can pack her in a jacket and blanket and push her for the trip. After four afternoons, she finally admits to herself that she's looking for Jim. On and off through the last few days, standing in front of the bathroom mirror with a toothbrush in her hand, trying to remember what it could possibly be for, she wonders if he's shaved since that first day or if maybe it's not scruff but the honest beginning of a beard. She wonders if he uses an electric razor on all the dogs, or if, for certain breeds, he might press his first two fingers together and slide them through the hair, snipping the ends with scissors like hair on a person's head. In the past four days he is the only person other than Leo that she has spoken with face to face. Margie's mother came for a week after the birth, and friends stopped by the second week, but now, in the fourth week, it's like the world has forgotten about her. Leo went back to work; her mother went home; her friends have moved on with their non-baby lives, either opting out of parenthood altogether or having children in their twenties like reasonable adults. She is thirty-eight and for the past fifteen years has managed the human resources department for a legal database company with a thousand-plus employees, and now she no longer knows how to use a toothbrush. She and Leo agreed she would take a year or two off when the baby was born, that her career would be there when she wanted to return. Margie wonders now why she would have agreed to such an arrangement, although leaving the baby is the only thing that sounds worse than staying where she is.

On Tuesday she loads Katherine into the stroller snuggled deep in a hat Margie knit herself, the needles balanced on her belly as the baby swelled inside her, as she waited impatiently for her old life to end. She and Katherine walk the few blocks to the park and find Jim sitting on the same bench they occupied together six days before. Margie's heart begins to pound. "Hey," he says when she passes, nodding his cigarette at the baby. "You guys must be on a routine." His beard is gone, replaced by a one-day growth.

Margie shields her hand to the sky, squinting toward the sun. "Why do you say that?"

"I see you walking by nearly every day at this time. I wondered when we'd run into each other again. I can't always get out at the same time. It depends on the dog."

"You've been watching us?" Margie is both elated and disturbed by this information. But hasn't she, too, been watching for him?

"Why don't you sit down."

Margie pauses for a moment, then settles herself onto the bench, instinctively hooking a foot through the stroller and rocking it back and forth.

"You're good with that baby," Jim says and leans forward. He puts a hand in the stroller for Katherine to sniff as if she were a dog. Margie holds her breath as he tickles Katherine's cheek, the baby's open mouth rooting back and forth in hopes of a nipple. Jim forms his hand into a dog's snout, the thumb clapping below the four flush fingers, and barks his hand at Kit Kat. "Woof." He settles back into the bench. "Where's her daddy?"

"Her what?" Margie says.

"Her dad."

"Oh, yes." She looks at Katherine and imagines Leo at work, finishing up e-mails for the day or leaning in the doorway of his office, arms crossed as he chats with a coworker or maybe just sitting at his desk staring blankly at the wall, nothing in a calm sea of nothing. "He isn't in the picture," she says. "He's gone." This doesn't feel like a lie to her. It is like Leo moves to another country every morning and, at the end of the day, moves home. Every day she worries she will hurt the child while Leo is at work, that the baby will be injured on her watch. Katherine will suddenly roll off the changing table or slip in the inch of bath water or overheat during a nap from too many layers or freeze to death from not enough or that Margie, from sheer exhaustion, will simply forget she is holding the baby and the baby will bounce to the floor. When Leo comes home he snuggles Katherine into his arm like a football, sits on the sofa, and slides off his shoes with the toe of the opposite foot. He asks Margie about her day and she sits next to her husband—aware in that moment it is ridiculous to think these things—and tells him it was fine. The next day it will start over again.

Jim shakes his head. "What fool man's going to leave a pretty little girl like you?" he says, and Margie feels her face heat before realizing he's talking to Katherine; of course he's talking to the baby.

Jim nods his head emphatically a few times. "She's going to be just fine without a daddy."

"My husband's at work," Margie says. "I don't know why I said that. He'll be home in less than an hour."

"That's what *you* think," Jim says. "It's a curse and a blessing, let me tell you. One day your baby grows up, puts on eye shadow, and looks at you like, who the fuck are you? Next thing you know, they live in Colorado while you're stuck bathing dogs in Nebraska."

"Why'd they move to Colorado?"

"Hell if I know." He takes another cigarette out of his pocket. She notes that it's not in the pack but just loose, and she thinks this tells her something about Jim, that he is a man who rations himself. She looks out at the park, the chilly metal of the slide reverberating in the air as a boy hits it repeatedly with a metal bat. *What is a boy doing loose with a metal bat?* she wonders, alarmed. She repositions the hat on Katherine's bald head, her eyes like black coins in their sockets. "Tell me about the dogs," she says, snuggling deeper in her coat.

Jim tells her about the different breeds—the intelligence of the border collie, the spunk of the beagle, how Chihuahuas get a bad rap as yappy dogs but in reality are some tough motherfuckers. "Sorry," he says and nods toward the stroller. "I shouldn't swear in front of the baby," unaware, Margie guesses, that he's been doing it all along.

"It's okay," she says. "She doesn't understand language." From the other direction three little leaguers and an overweight man in pleated khakis and a gray sweatshirt make their way toward the boy with the bat. "Sometimes," she begins, "when the baby is crying, I'll lean over her crib and just watch her cry." The boy throws down the bat and begins running. Margie can watch Katherine cry and feel like she did in delivery, such an overwhelming sense of emptiness that it's almost like being filled up. "It's like I'm watching it on TV," she says. "Like she's not a real baby in the room."

"You should get a basset hound," Jim says. "It'd be good for you and that little girl."

"I'm just so tired." The day is ending, the sun beginning its descent, which means the night will start soon. Margie will get her half-hour of making dinner, then the ten minutes to eat it while she and Leo eat in shifts, and then the baby will start to cry and cry and cry.

Jim slaps his hands on his knees and stands. "I should get back to work. Those dogs aren't going to bathe themselves." He bends over and gives Margie a kiss just above the corner of her mouth and it's like being released from a trance, a dream.

"That's not appropriate," she says, her voice an echo.

"It's okay," he says. "The baby's sleeping," and sure enough, she is, her fist bare and red escaped from the blanket, coiled like an internal organ or a snake.

"I love her, you know," Margie says. She laughs, or tries to. "What I said earlier? About watching her? I was just talking."

"Maybe you're not ready for a dog."

Tears push into Margie's eyes. This happens all the time now—it is nothing new—but like every time, she really means it. "You don't think I'm ready for a dog?"

"You'd better get that baby home," he says and pulls his collar up against the cold as he twists his last cigarette under his boot. "But come back tomorrow. I'll have a surprise for you."

That night around ten, Margie's stomach clenches at the first sound of Katherine stirring in her crib, her bleating cry echoing through the monitor. Dirty dinner dishes sit in the kitchen; a pile of unfolded baby clothes rests by the stairs. It isn't so much that Margie is exhausted to the point where she can't stay up for an hour rocking the baby, or even two hours. It's not knowing when it will end. What if Katherine cries until three this time, or four? Or dawn? Will she stop tomorrow night, or is this now Margie's life for the next two months or six years or forever? Leo says, "I'll take first shift," and makes his way upstairs, coming back with the baby, her large eyes blinking against the light.

"I can do it," Margie says and pushes herself to sitting on the sofa.

"Get some sleep," Leo says running a finger against Katherine's cheek, and Margie feels a spark of anger shoot through her.

"Let me," she says and stands up, taking the baby in her arms. Instantly she wants to give her back. She hates this constant pushing and pulling. During the day, when the baby finally naps, she feels an overwhelming sense of relief, complicated immediately by the need to hear her cry, to know that she is still alive. In the beginning she would lay Katherine in her crib upstairs, but the sound of the floorboards creaking would wake her, so now Margie lays her on the carpeted living room floor and sits next to her, her hands in constant motion as she loops yarn around the knitting needles. This constant push and pull, it reminds her of men she dated back in graduate school—she has a master's degree, in management!—who would reject her, then love her, then reject her again. She worries there's a reason Leo wants first shift—some golden reason she's overlooked—and just in case, she doesn't want him to have it. Isn't having a baby supposed to make one selfless? Here she is, exactly the opposite, a greedy mother who wants first shift, knowing Leo is as tired as she. This baby, the one in her arms, was conceived the night they rented a porno from the cable company for $9.95. It was supposed to be something light-hearted and adventurous, but it ended up being a complicated hour of copycat that resembled a badly choreographed dance routine they weren't in shape for. They were charged three times for the movie, and she wondered if it was even a mistake or if the cable company counted on her being too embarrassed to call and complain. Thirty dollars later, they had a baby on the way. How is she supposed to handle a baby when she couldn't even handle their cable bill? The last time they had sex was weeks ago in an attempt to induce labor, a slippery, mechanical affair in which she kept on her sports bra and Leo his socks and shoes. Socks she could understand, but *shoes*? She is just so tired. What if they never have sex again, or worse, what if they do?

She moves back to the couch, the baby still in her arms, although Margie feels Katherine slipping further down her stomach. "Here," Leo says. "Your shift's over." He takes the baby from Margie even as she says no, her arms holding the baby out like an offering, even as she lays her head down on a pillow and falls asleep.

The next day Jim arrives with Beulah, a black-and-grey-speckled Great Dane that prances with the grace of a ballerina yet weighs nearly as much as Jim.

"I don't introduce her to just anybody," he says. "But I thought you might appreciate her."

Margie doesn't know what she's done to deserve this praise. "Thank you," she says, resting a hand on the dog's back, patting her like she would a couch cushion. "That means a lot to me."

Jim snaps his fingers, and Beulah sits down on her delicate haunches, her ears pricked, her eyes on Jim's fingers. Beulah follows Jim's hand into the folds of his pants pocket from which he pulls out a dog treat shaped like a miniature T-bone in bright red and white. "Here," he says to Margie. "Give her this. You'll be friends for life."

Margie takes the treat and holds it out; Beulah nibbles it from around her fingers, then taps Margie's hand with her nose so she'll release the rest of the bite. Beulah gobbles it down without chewing, then swoops her long tongue against Margie's hand, the texture of gardening gloves, wet but pleasant.

Jim leans back—the apron he's wearing today is cleaner than usual—and takes his first of two cigarettes from his pocket and lights it. He exhales, and while Margie isn't sure, it appears to her he has leaned forward slightly to blow it in the stroller.

"Beulah spends her days at the salon with me keeping tabs on the other dogs. I like to imagine her with a little clipboard, making sure Olive's got her time in the run and Dinga's fed on schedule." Margie likes that Jim imagines his dog with a clipboard. It reminds her of the ridiculous outfits celebrities put their pets in, and she would not have guessed she would see any connection between Jim and these spoiled Hollywood kids, but there it is. She needs to remind herself not to judge people, to not make so many snap decisions.

"Why is it you don't see your kids anymore?" she asks.

Jim strokes Beulah's neck, a touch the big dog leans toward. "I love dogs like a politician loves money, but not like they've got them at Trudy's. Who would drop off someone for a haircut at eight in the morning if the appointment isn't until three? It's an insult to the dogs. They're supposed to be locked in cages the whole day until we can get to them. I go near crazy with them locked up like that." He runs his finger in a circle in front of himself. "Some days I let them run loose up front in the lobby. What do I care? I don't own the place. I just work there."

"There's nothing wrong with that," Margie says, but who knows? Maybe there is. Margie thinks of the dogs running loose at Jim's feet, twisting and turning at his ankles. She wonders how many he has at a time and if there's any way they are as loud as Katherine, who wails at such a decibel, with such consistency, Margie sometimes stands out on the porch, careful not to lock the door, the sound dampened behind her but not gone. Growing up, her family never listened to the radio or had the TV on during the day, and Margie was smothered daily in silence. Even Leo walks around in stocking feet, careful to shut cupboards slowly, but there is nothing to be done with Katherine.

"My kids?" Jim says. "Their mother's just doing what she thinks is right. We got divorced a long time ago, a shitty deal, and it just got so I missed those kids so bad I did something stupid."

Katherine whimpers in her stroller, her mouth jangling back and forth. "She's hungry," Margie says. "I should feed her."

"Of course she is," Jim says. "Babies are always hungry." He settles back on the bench hooking his elbows behind him, one elbow—the left one—only an inch away from Margie.

"Do you mind?" she says and puts her hands to the zipper of her windbreaker, her heart pounding.

"You do what you have to." Margie takes her nursing cover from the diaper bag—the cover is called a "hooter hider," yet another humiliation geared toward motherhood—and secures it around her neck before reaching for Katherine. "See, that's the difference between men and women," Jim says, as if that explains it all. "All I wanted," he continues, "was to see my kids. See what they looked like sleeping. I'd forgotten, you know? That happens. You don't think it will, but it does." He looks out at the park; it's gotten colder since they've been meeting, on and off for a few weeks now. Just this morning Margie looked at the calendar and was shocked to see it was time to make Katherine's two-month checkup. "You and that husband of yours ever break it off, be sure you let him see her. Don't hold that baby hostage."

Margie feels a surge of panic at the idea Leo could leave, that she will be responsible for raising this baby all alone. "I wouldn't do that," she says. "Besides, that's not going to happen."

"You say that now," he says. "Same thing with these dogs. People get to thinking, 'what a cute little puppy,' but next thing you know, that cute little puppy's shitting all over the floor and they're carting her to the hair salon for a sixty-dollar haircut."

"It really costs that much? Sixty dollars?"

Jim nods. "And we're competitive. That's just your run-of-the-mill cut. Did you know you can give a dog a perm?" He shakes his head. "Ridiculous. People ought to just let a dog be a dog, a man be a man."

Margie feels the familiar tug on her breast that indicates Katherine's done, that she's moved from eating to grazing. She pulls the baby from beneath the cover, embarrassed to see a drop of milk roll down Katherine's chin, something so utterly personal.

Across the street, a woman in a zebra-striped coat approaches the door to Trudy's, tugs on it, finds it locked, then looks around for an explanation. "She's got a dalmatian," Jim says. "I think she got it to match the coat. Remember when that movie came out, the one with all the dalmatians? People brought those puppies home like it was their job, and the kennels were full of them two months later. They're hyper and insecure. People weren't prepared for that." He stands up and makes a clicking noise with his tongue; Beulah rolls off her haunches and onto her feet.

"Maybe I'm a dalmatian," she jokes.

"You're more of a pug," Jim says, and she has no idea how to take this but decides, in the moment, to take it as a compliment.

That night Margie falls into bed exhausted, the list in her head writing itself: dishes, laundry, bottles to be washed. She used to go to bed thinking of adult things like her job for some company or another, or what was going on in the world. Weren't they due to vote on a president soon, and wasn't that a big deal? Leo puts a hand on the edge of her hip. "Another week," he says, dancing his fingers forward.

Margie's body tenses, the quiet in the house like a shadow.

The next morning as Katherine takes her nap on the living room floor, Margie tiptoes out of the room to the foyer, shuts the door behind her, and walks to the mailbox. Outside, she listens to the sounds of the birds in the cool fall air. She has the baby monitor in her hand, turned low so the sound is like an echo of static, and in the distance, perhaps a few blocks away, she hears the howl of a single dog. She collects the mail—mostly bills—and heads back to the house. She puts her hand on the knob and turns but the knob doesn't budge. The lock. She left it secured.

Panic lights like wildfire through her chest and arms as she puts the monitor to her ear, the sound like white noise. She imagines Katherine rolling onto her stomach for the first time and choking. Katherine smothering to death in the blanket. Katherine piercing an eye with a knitting needle. Margie crawls over the boxwood shrubs in front of the living room, scratching her arms, dropping the monitor in the dirt, hoping to catch a glimpse of Katherine. How is it she ever thought her daughter didn't have a personality? The baby is still on her back, the blanket undisturbed, her eyes closed. But is she breathing? Margie knocks her fist loudly against the glass and Katherine startles awake, her head and arms vibrating side-to-side, before her mouth screws into a scream toward the ceiling.

Margie feels another shot of adrenaline make its way through her heart. If she calls the police it'll remain on a permanent record, something that will one day be reported to Children's Services. Her neighbor Mrs. Tamara has a key, but already Margie feels Mrs. Tamara's disapproval at the way she takes Katherine out in the cold every day, the weather hovering just above freezing. Leo works nearly an hour away in Omaha in his cocoon of silence, and besides, she has no phone. The back door is always locked. There is no other way in the house. Her mind jumps to Jim—*I just wanted to see them sleep*—and already her legs are in motion, picking up momentum as she runs down the street, turning at the curb for the park. It's a run she can make with her eyes closed, so many times she's pushed Katherine down these very sidewalks.

Even before she reaches for the handle she hears the noise inside Trudy's, the cacophony of dogs. "Shut the door!" Jim yells from the back and Margie slips inside and throws her weight against the door. There are six or seven dogs roaming around the front—some up to her waist, others circling her heels. "Shut!" she yells back. The salon is warm and humid after the bitter cold of outside, the smell of wet dogs and shampoo overwhelming. It is a lush salon with a cheetah sofa in the waiting area, only instead of magazines about hairdos there are magazines about dogs. Instead of salon chairs, there are shiny silver tables, each positioned in front of its own mirror rimmed with Hollywood lights. A blonde cocker spaniel makes his way to Margie and nudges her leg with his nose; instinctively Margie puts down her hand for the dog to sniff.

Jim peeks out from behind two velvet pink curtains separating the salon area from the back room. "I'll be out in a second," he says, no surprise in his voice at seeing Margie.

A moment later he comes to the front counter, the cocker now in Margie's arms as she explains that she locked herself out. Jim looks around, scratching his head. He asks about the baby and Margie tells him that Katherine's inside alone, right there next to the knitting needles. He points to the cocker spaniel. "He's been here since last Friday. That's three days. What are people thinking?" He moves to the front door and flips the Open sign to Closed. "Let me grab some things."

A moment later he reappears from behind the velvet curtains with his coat on and Beulah secured by a leash. "I'll just be a moment, girls. You sit tight." The dogs whine as if they understand, and perhaps, Margie thinks, they do.

She's surprisingly calm walking home with Jim and Beulah, as if it were a day for outrageous things to happen—a baby alone in a house, a dog this big—but still a day she will never turn into an anecdote. On the porch Jim takes a leather glove from his pocket and slips it on. She assumes this is to cover his fingerprints, which strikes her as ridiculous, and only after he breaks the front window does she realize it's to protect his hand. She had assumed he would have a lock-picking set, some kind of master key or system. It had not occurred to her to simply break the glass.

Jim reaches in and unlocks the door from the inside. "Here you go."

There's a catch as the door swings open, a pregnant moment full of silence. Margie knocks Jim out of her way as she bounds through the foyer to her baby. Katherine is on her back, her arms and legs splayed, her head lolled to one side. Margie scoops up her child—careful to cradle her head—and pulls her to her chest. It's like they've been separated forever, as if the time before the baby existed was another lifetime.

The baby's eyes are puffy from crying herself to sleep; they flutter awake and then close again.

Jim knocks on the doorframe with a knuckle, Beulah behind him. "She okay?"

Margie nods her head, unwilling to move her mouth from the baby's soft, warm neck to speak the words. Jim looks around the living room. "It's a nice house you got here." She looks around at all the knickknacks that will need to be removed once the baby starts walking, at the shelves of books she'll never find time to read. That morning she awoke a half hour early to start a batch of chili in the Crock-Pot, their first genuinely home-cooked meal in almost two months. The smell is now making its way through the house, the warm spice of winter in the air.

"I don't know how to thank you," she says.

Beulah nudges past Jim and lifts her front paws onto the sofa, pushing herself delicately onto the couch. "She sleeps in the bed with me too," he says. "We eat dinner together on the couch and sleep in the same bed." Margie imagines the weight of this dog would be like another person beside you. "Beulah," Jim says. "Little Beau." He snaps his fingers and Beulah unfolds her long limbs and climbs down from the sofa.

"I should get back to work," he says and stands there a moment awkwardly. Cold air is starting to make its way into the living room from the broken window and Margie reaches for the afghan on the back of a chair. She learned to knit in her third trimester, her neighbor Mrs. Tamara coming over in the afternoons to teach her how, switching from hot tea to iced as the summer grew warmer. "I knit for my own babies," Mrs. Tamara said. "Every baby needs a little homemade love." For the rest of her life, the sound of knitting needles clacking together will be a sound Margie associates with Katherine, a sound she will recognize out of context and always know.

"Thank you again," she says, and because she knows this will please Jim even more than the compliment, she says it to Beulah and not him.

That evening after dinner Leo takes Katherine into the living room and settles in front of the PlayStation as Margie starts a kettle for tea, gearing up for the colicky night ahead. A knock on the back door startles her so badly she nearly knocks the two mugs to the floor. She moves back the curtain and sees Jim's face outlined in the darkness, the blonde cocker spaniel in his arms.

She lets the curtain drop back in place and opens the door, pushing Jim and the dog down the step so she can stand next to him and close the door. "What are you doing here?" When Leo got home she told him some kids were playing baseball in the street, that an errant ball shattered the glass. Before he arrived she taped two layers of cardboard over the pane, then called a window company to come for an estimate.

"I got fired today," Jim says. "That bitch with the dalmatian called and ratted me out. Trudy showed up while I was here, and there were eight dogs running loose. They'd torn up her cheetah couch." He pets the cocker spaniel's head. "Whose dumb idea was it to decorate a dog salon with a cat, I asked her, and she told me to pack my shit." He holds the dog out, the cocker's nubby tail thumping against Jim's wrist. "Brought you a present."

He moves the dog to Margie's arms. She resists, but he lets go, forcing her to hug the dog to her. "I can't keep a dog," she says. "What about Katherine?" Jim bows his head and kisses the blonde dog on the forehead, where a white patch of hair is shaped like a star. He turns toward the alley. "You can't leave me with this dog," Margie says, holding the dog out. "How am I supposed to take care of a baby and a dog?"

Jim laughs, and Beulah emerges from the shadows where she's been waiting patiently next to the garage, his faithful companion. "I was wrong before about the basset hound," Jim says. "You're a cocker spaniel girl. I should have seen it right away." He waves a hand as he disappears out of the circle of their porch light, and it occurs to Margie she has no way to trace him, that he will most likely never return to the park. The teakettle whistles and she steps back into the kitchen and turns off the stove, removing the kettle with her empty hand, the dog still clutched to her chest.

"Marge?" Leo shouts from the living room. "Were you talking to someone?"

She pauses, then puts the dog on the ground, his feet and nails scurrying to find footing on the linoleum. He finds it and shoots toward the sound of Leo's voice.

"What the—" Leo starts then stops. "Whose dog is this?" he says even louder. Margie follows the dog into the living room. The cocker spaniel has climbed up the side of Leo's leg to the baby and is trying desperately to lick her face; Leo holds the baby with one arm, the dog at bay with the other. Kat's eyes shoot open, her face screwed tight in an immediate scream. "I've always wanted a dog," Margie says.

Leo holds the dog back by the neck, the dog's wet nose straining toward Katherine to get another lick. Katherine wails, her cries echoing off the walls and ceiling as Margie's breasts let down with milk. "Where'd this dog come from?"

Margie can imagine Jim and Beulah making their way back down the alley, a man and his horse walking into the sunset, no matter that it's already dark. "A friend dropped him off."

Leo lifts Katherine above his head, the dog's body in constant motion as he strains to lick the child. "When's she picking it up?"

Margie plucks Katherine from her husband's arms. "I don't think he is." She pulls Katherine against her sodden shirt, the baby's legs kicking into the soft bread of Margie's stomach. Katherine doesn't stop crying, even as she wraps her fingers around her mother's thumb, as Margie tilts her head to the side so Katherine can bury her face in her neck, the sound absorbed by Margie's body.

"What the hell are we going to do with a dog?" Leo says as Margie moves her dinner bowl from the ottoman to the floor, the dish smeared with leftover chili. The dog breaks away from Leo's grasp and begins licking the bowl at Margie's feet, his large pink tongue contouring itself to the edges, a swath of white dish left in its wake. Margie imagines Jim and Beulah on their way home, the soft-shoe sound of Beulah's paws. It is almost bedtime. She would bet money that Beulah sleeps with her head on a pillow, and that because no one is watching, Jim spoons his belly against her back. Katherine's cry turns into a yawn. She will go down soon for the night and awaken an hour later, screaming. The cocker spaniel sits, his legs quivering in hopes of more food. Margie kisses the top of Katherine's head as she bends to pick up the bowl, the dish once dirty, now clean.

I Don't Live in This Town

The high school marching band plays a stilted rendition of "Grand Old Flag," slightly off-key but loud enough to be effective. Milo wanders the streets of Corbett, Oregon, following the clanging noise. He himself played the oboe for a year before giving it up, even though he liked the instrument—the sweetness of the reed; the windy, low, sad sound the oboe made when he blew. He was bad at picking the keys—his fingers in the middle of a growth spurt, gangly and longer than he was used to—but he kept with it until his father, in a mood one night, complained about the screeching neighborhood dogs. Although on other nights, in better moods, Milo's father encouraged him.

People in the crowd wave small, waxy American flags they've purchased at a stand to commemorate the Fourth. Milo steps off the curb in front of an old man in loose, worn Levis and a ratty white T-shirt, and stops to watch the parade. He's glad to be away from his parents and younger sister for the day, still immersed in a crowd but an anonymous one. They've agreed to meet at sundown by the Live Beef Raffle where Milo will drive them back to camp—his parents will have been drinking—for another night of sleeping on the ground. He feels like an old man already at seventeen—his back acting up, shuttling his family in a minivan from one display of The Old West to the next. Four days into the family vacation and his mother has already crammed the van half-full with stuff: a two-foot tree stump chainsawed into the shape of a bear, a kit the size of a filing cabinet to grow her own bees. Milo knows he's too old for a family vacation—his mother antiquing, his father constantly grumbling about how Milo's leading his life, his sister a depressed fifteen-year-old with a constant can of Diet Coke in her hand. The night before they left, his father stood over a map of the Northwest and said emphatically, "Idaho, Washington, Oregon," his finger punctuating each state on the map. "This is the family we've got and the vacation we've planned."

"Why do we have to go anywhere?" his sister, Ali, whined.

"It's America," his father said evenly. "We go anywhere because we can." Milo's heard enough stories from his father's childhood—the scrimping and saving, the other boys' teasing, washing the same shirt night after night in the bathroom sink just to wear it to school again the next day. His father has worked hard to lift himself out of that, to pack more than ten shirts in the closet and become like everyone else, and there's no way Milo's getting out of this one-week cross-country American Dream.

The band marches by in their mismatched T-shirts—no oboes certainly, only the standard small-town instruments like saxophones, snare drums, all the girls on flutes. The band is trailed by a rusted antique pickup truck from the 1930s pulling a hayrack with six bundles of hay and a large painted sign that reads "Prom Court." There are three sets of adolescent boys and girls, with the couple at the front wearing a tiara and a crown. The king is muscular—most likely a jock in football and basketball—while the queen appears so thin she will break. Her hair is dyed a brassy blonde to match her yellow gown, and even from the street, Milo can see tracks beginning to run in her makeup, little rivulets of sweat that help assure him she isn't a doll. Over the summer he's forgotten how beautiful high school girls can be—their skin tan and radiant, their bodies like slashes of perfection riding down the street on bales of hay. But it is the boy on the back hay bale that catches Milo's attention. He is thinner than the others—narrow through the shoulders with long legs and arms that seem to hang off the sides of his body like sticks. He is wearing a tuxedo and sits stiffly, his posture unnaturally straight for a teenager, his dark hair curling onto his forehead above eyes that appear black at a distance. As the truck drives closer, Milo sees that they're brown. That his nose is too big for his delicate face, and that acne scars line his jawbone like a map of Hawaii. Milo looks at the girl next to him on the hay bale; she's wearing a minty-green dress the color of a grasshopper cocktail. The right spaghetti strap keeps slipping, and Milo watches as the boy continually takes his long index finger and runs the strap slowly back up her shoulder. She turns to him and smiles every time.

The float turns a corner and Milo walks down the sidewalk, stopping at an open-air stand to buy a peach and a handful of cherries, spitting the pits into a Kleenex as he goes. He continues down to the high school where the parade has stopped. The band kids are unloading their instruments in front of the Corbett Cardinals gymnasium, not caring that the rented tubas slide across the ground collecting dirt, that a clarinet is abandoned in the wet grass. One overweight sophomore stops and tugs miserably at his T-shirt, pulling it away from his large body where thick lines of sweat from the bass drum have X'ed his back. Milo finds the homecoming float and the tall boy with the dark, curly hair. He's already separated himself from the group, the girl in the mint dress staring at him forlornly as he walks away, his head high and his shoulders square, looking beautifully out of place among the backdrop of the high school, the teachers running around trying to organize the volunteers to help with the spaghetti feed later that night. All you can eat for four dollars, including garlic bread, salad, and dessert.

Milo walks quickly to catch up with the other boy. "I'm Milo," he says, and holds out his hand. For a moment, he expects the boy to take it in his and kiss it, a slight bend to his knee, but the boy merely stares at Milo's hand for a moment before shaking it.

"Toby," he says, and nods to the street. "Pretty corny, huh. All this parade shit."

Milo smiles. "We have parades in Missoula too. It's not that weird."

"You moved here from Montana?" Toby asks.

Milo debates for a moment but doesn't correct him to say he's only here for the day. "Yeah," he says. "From Montana." Who's to say he can't move here from Missoula, decide on a lark to start a new life? He's seventeen, almost an adult. In another year, when he finishes high school, he can move wherever he wants. He told his dad the night before they left for vacation that he wasn't going to go to college but that he'd stay in Missoula and clean pools with his buddy Tim. His father was furious, saying he didn't want Milo hanging out with Tim anymore, and why, goddamn it, was he so set on making life hard? Milo hasn't actually talked to Tim about the business but knows he himself would be good at the books as well as the labor. Maybe he'll move to New York and be an artist or to Pittsburgh to work in a steel mill. Do they still have steel mills, he wonders. They must; everyone still needs steel.

Toby runs a hand though his dense hair. "That's cool. I've lived in Corbett my whole life. I'm moving next year, though, to go to college."

"That's cool," Milo echoes. He looks down, shuffling his sandaled feet. A layer of dust settles on Toby's shiny black rentals.

"Have you checked out the games downtown yet?" Toby asks.

"Not yet. What do they have?"

Toby shrugs. "Ring tosses, pie eating, nothing too cool." He pauses. "You want to go?"

Milo feels something flare inside him, a brief spark of excitement. "Sure. What about the girl though, the one in the grasshopper dress?"

Toby laughs and looks over at her; she's been watching them but quickly looks away. "She'll live."

They walk downtown, Toby still in his tuxedo looking comfortable with only a thin line of perspiration above his upper lip, while Milo sweats in nothing more than a golf shirt. They stop at a stand and pay fifty cents for five chances to pop balloons on a wall with a dart. Both lose. "I've got terrible coordination," Milo admits and Toby only laughs like this is an endearing quality, not a weakness as his father would have him believe. Milo wonders where his parents are, or his sister, and whether they can see him. He hopes not. He doesn't want them bursting on the scene and ruining this for him, telling Toby they're merely passing through on vacation and won't be back.

"Where do you live?" Toby asks and Milo shrugs his shoulders.

"That way." He points to the left.

Toby nods and doesn't question it further. "Do you want to get a beer?"

Milo looks up. They're standing in front of the beer garden, the smell of charred meat heavy in the air. "You think you can get us some?"

"My dad runs the bar in town and they're sponsoring the beer garden. He'd kill me if he found out, but one of the waitresses will sneak us some." He looks down at his tux. "I should change first, you mind?"

Milo doesn't mind at all.

Milo and Toby walk the few blocks to Toby's house and Toby asks him to wait in the living room while he bounds up the stairs, two at a time. Compared to Milo's own house, Toby's is surprisingly uncluttered—no little figurines of dogs or fat, glowing children in pastels. Milo's mother is constantly buying things, creating a life so busy it must be full. A newspaper is strewn across the kitchen floor and an orange kitten no bigger than two fists comes mewing out of the corner where she's been sleeping on a sweatshirt, swaying side to side as if drunk. "Hey, buddy," Milo says and sits on the newspaper. She scrabbles onto his knee, digging her sharp, new claws into the flesh leaving tiny droplets of blood.

"I see you've met Max," Toby says and sits next to Milo on the floor, reaching over his lap to pet the cat. "Maxine, actually." He looks more ordinary now, dressed in khaki cuttoffs and a T-shirt that reads "The Rusty Nail," a name Milo recognizes from the beer garden. His hair seems less debonair, his thin arms pale and freckled without the sleek lines of the tuxedo jacket to hide them. "We just got her a few days ago," Toby says and nods toward the cat. "Hey, Max," he coos and reaches again across Milo's lap to stroke her enormous head. The cat instantly begins purring, vibrating against Milo's thigh.

"She's nice."

"We had a cat die a few months ago and my mom went completely crazy." Toby points to a dark-green-and-black ceramic pot above the fridge. "That's Max Number One."

"You keep the ashes in the kitchen?"

"We didn't know what else to do with him. The kitchen makes as much sense as anywhere. My dad put a cigarette out in him one time, in the urn. I thought my mom was going to go ballistic." Toby laughs and Milo joins in although he doesn't think it's funny.

"I'm moving to New Mexico next year," Milo says. "My dad wants me learn pottery." Toby only stares at him. "You want to go back to the parade?" Milo asks. "Get some beer?"

"We can do that if you want." Toby turns to the fridge and reaches his long arm to open the door. "We might have some here." Sure enough, there's an open twelve pack of Labatts in the fridge and he takes out two cans and hands one to Milo. "My folks don't have any idea how much beer's in here at one time. They wouldn't notice if we drank the rest of the twelve."

Milo follows Toby into the living room where they sit on opposite sides of the couch. Toby puts his feet up on the ottoman and switches on the TV; Milo puts his feet next to Toby's. He sips his beer and coughs a bit in his hand. Milo drinks more than his parents think. He and Tim sometimes drink on Friday nights when his parents believe he's at the movies or a high school football game, or on the weekends when he and Tim are supposed to be cleaning pools for Tim's dad. They drink in Tim's parents' tool shed, then sometimes, if Tim's in a good mood, they'll lay down on one of his father's wool blankets and touch each other. Toby doesn't remind Milo of Tim at all. He seems gentler, with those locks of dark hair hovering above his eyes, the way he gazes soulfully at the TV. Maybe he should open the pool-cleaning business with Toby—just the two of them, the sun, and an ocean full of water if you add the pools together. He's too shy to make the first move, knowing that if he has read Toby wrong, he might get yelled at or hit, rumors started. Then he remembers: I don't live in this town. His hand moves between them, inching its way toward Toby as if on its own accord.

Toby stands quickly. "You want another? I could get us another." Milo is certain, suddenly, that Toby has invited him here only for beer.

"I should be getting back to the parade," Milo says and sits up at the edge of the couch, his knees firmly together.

"Do you want to try and get beer there?"

Milo shrugs. "We can try, if you think it'll work." Toby sits back down and stares straight ahead. He pauses a moment then stands again and takes both empty cans in his large hand as he walks past the ottoman. He squeezes closer to Milo to brush against his leg and trail his empty hand across Milo's arm on his way to the kitchen. Perhaps Milo hasn't read this incorrectly after all.

At the beer garden, Milo hovers outside trying to look inconspicuous as Toby goes in for beer. The streets are full—people milling around in tank tops and shorts, with plastic, foaming cups of beer even though the sign clearly states: "Cigarettes and Alcoholic Beverages are only allowed in the Beer Garden." A woman in garish lipstick laughs and leans against the man she's with, a stoic type in a black cowboy hat and boots despite the heat. Toby comes back with two Styrofoam to-go cups with lids. "Success," he says and hands one to Milo.

Milo takes a sip of tepidly warm beer through the opening of the lid. Even though he knows it's beer, he expects from the container that it will be the acrid taste of coffee, a taste he's still acquiring. "Thanks."

They walk through the throngs of people, Milo with an eye out for his family. He sees his sister, Ali, sitting on a street curb by herself in an Atari tank top tied at the waist, her dyed-black hair piled high in an intricate sculpture of plastic barrettes and hairspray. She's nibbling the breading off a corn dog, and Milo looks away quickly but it's too late. She waves to him and comes over, shuffling her green Chucks across the concrete as she throws the pink meat of the corndog in the garbage. "Hey," she says and looks inquiringly at Toby. "Who's your friend?"

Toby takes a sip from his cup then tells her his name.

"Hey," Ali says and pushes her black bangs out of her eyes.

"Hey." Toby responds. "Milo said you guys just moved into town."

She looks at her brother and raises her eyebrows. "He did? Where did he say we're living?" Ali crosses her arms at the elbows and stares at Milo who pleads with his eyes that she not blow his cover. I am a citizen of Corbett, he thinks.

"Over there," Toby says and points to the east.

"That's true," she says. "We do live in that direction." Milo lets out a sigh of relief. When he least expects it, his sister will come through for him. A few months ago he came home with a bruised mouth, his eyes glossy from pot, and she told their mother the next morning that Milo was up sick all night, vomiting in the toilet. When he came down looking haggard and drawn later that afternoon, Bette merely brushed a hand over his head at the table and asked if he wanted some ginger ale.

"You want a beer?" Toby asks and Ali says, "Yeah, if you can get one."

"Thanks," Milo says to Ali as Toby shuffles to the beer garden.

"Why would you say we live in a shithole like this?" she says and Milo just shrugs his shoulders. "Never mind, I don't want to know." She fans her face with her hand. "Have you seen Mom and Dad?"

"Nope."

"Me either, thank god."

Toby comes back with another three cups and passes them around. "We should probably steal from my house on the next round, I don't want to push my luck."

While they're walking down the confetti-strewn street, Milo grabs Ali's arm lightly and whispers in her ear, "Leave."

"You can't tell me what to do," she says and shakes his hand away. She looks back at the main street, her face collapsing. "I don't have anyone to hang out with."

"Find Mom and Dad."

"Oh, right. That sounds like a lot of fun. They're probably off antiquing or singing 'God Damn Bless America.'"

"Please," Milo says softly, and Ali stops walking.

"I think I'm going to head back to town," she says loudly, and Toby stops and turns around.

"You sure?"

"Yeah, I was already a little drunk when I met up with you guys."

Milo knows from the sweet, doughy smell of her breath she wasn't—that she's probably eaten nothing but corndogs and miniature donuts all afternoon—and feels a pang of affection for his sister. Sometimes late on weekend nights she comes home looking like a warrior dressed in a push-up bra and nylons, thick eyeliner ringing her eyes and lipstick gumming on her lips. Five minutes later, padding down the hall to her bedroom from the bathroom—her face shiny and clean and wearing nothing but a long T-shirt and boxers—she'll look as innocent and fresh-faced

as a six-year-old, the transformation shocking Milo into the real-
ization his sister is as breakable as he.

Milo and Toby head back to Toby's house, grab the rest of the
beers from Toby's fridge—nine in all—and shove them in a backpack and head back downtown. The sun is beginning to set, a
golden-red tinge to the sky. Hard rock music from the beer garden
is floating out from Main Street along with the smell of old grease
frying. The two boys walk around town, ducking into alleys to refill
their cups and crush the cans to put back in Toby's backpack. "You
want to see the school?" Toby asks.

Milo follows him under the pale streetlights, too far apart to completely light the street. What is there to see, he thinks? There probably hasn't been a crime in this town since it was born, nothing
more harmful than two teenage boys walking around with a backpack full of beer on a summer night. He's starting to feel drunk, a
little woozy in his motions. He feels like he's beginning to move
through water: a slow, warm feeling surrounding him, pulsing out
like so much light.

Toby goes to the front of the school to a high window with mesh
wiring inside and jumps high enough to swing in the window, obviously unlocked. "Here. Give me a boost." Milo cups his hands in
front of a sign for the Corbett Cards, the "C" in Cards spray-painted
over and replaced with a "T." Toby steps in, light as cotton it seems,
as Milo swings his hands up so Toby can grasp the ledge.

"Are we going to get in trouble?" Milo asks.

Toby locks his elbows in the window and looks back at Milo—
"Do you want to?"—then slides out of reach. He reappears a
moment later at the back door and lets Milo in. He grabs a basketball from a large wire bucket on wheels and throws it at Milo, the
sound echoing like gunshots as it bounces in the empty gym. Milo
lets it pass, the dribbles quickening and growing softer, rolling
finally until the ball is still. "I'll show you where my locker is."

"Are you in summer school?"

"Not the dumb kind," Toby says quickly. "College prep." Milo thinks fleetingly of his father—his ultimatum that Milo will be kicked out of the house if he doesn't apply to college, if he doesn't finally become the son Carter wants him to be. "I'm handing you life on a goddamn platter," his father always says. "And you're telling me you're too full to eat?" He thinks of all the minutes and hours he's wasted on geometry and economics. On the history of a world he's certain he doesn't occupy.

They walk the halls, their footsteps squeaking on the linoleum, the smell of wax and paint clogging the air. The halls are long and thin like Milo's school in Missoula, only with no graffiti, not a lick. He's never seen a high school so clean. The lockers are institutional green, or appear to be in the faded light coming in from the windows. Toby stops in front of a locker and fiddles with the combination then opens it. There are textbooks inside that Milo recognizes from his freshman year, a *Sports Illustrated* calendar, and a picture of a red Porsche taped on the inside of the door. Pencils and pens roll precariously on the top shelf. "I guess it's not that exciting." Toby stands there with one arm on the door.

Milo leans in so their bodies are close but still not touching. He looks into Toby's eyes—black again in the waning light—to make sure it's okay, then runs a hand slowly from Toby's collarbone to his belly. He feels as much as hears the intake of breath.

Toby moves his thin neck down toward Milo, reminding Milo of an ostrich. "I've never kissed another guy before," he whispers.

"It's like kissing a girl," Milo says. "Only better."

Sometime later—Milo can't even guess how much time has elapsed—they crawl through the gymnasium window one after the other and reenter the street dance. The band, Hard Knocks, is a group of long-haired guys in their thirties and forties who do construction or farming on the weekdays. They belt their way through Motley Crüe's "Smoking in the Boy's Room" with too much bass and too much air guitar from the lead singer. Milo wants desperately to hold Toby's hand, to keep that warm feeling going. When the band finishes the song the drunk crowd erupts, and the lead singer smiles despite his cool-boy demeanor as they slide into the next song.

Milo sees his father looming large in the crowd, dancing with a woman who is prettier than his mother, her arms wrapped around his father's neck with her fingers crossed at the back, a smile on his dad's face as if this is his real life: a pretty girl, rock and roll music, dancing with the sway of the crowd. One of Milo's biggest worries is that the entire world, what he's supposed to be working his way toward, is just like high school.

"Want another beer?" Toby says, but Milo shakes his head. He knows if he has one more he'll begin to spin, the world losing its soft focus as he careens out of control. "I'll be right back," Toby says. He stands there dumbly for a moment then weaves his way through the crowd.

A few yards away, the woman snakes her hands down from Carter's neck to around his midsection, squeezing herself against him. She throws her head back and laughs as Milo's father looks side to side, most likely looking for his wife. He catches Milo's eye and hooks him a wave but Milo just stares back. He's pretty sure his parents don't love each other the way they're supposed to.

Toby returns with the beer trailed by a meaty adolescent boy Milo recognizes from the hayride. He's changed out of his tuxedo into a Chicago Bulls basketball jersey and jean jacket, although he's still wearing his crown. "Is this your little friend?" he says to Toby and pokes Milo hard in the collarbone with more pressure than Milo would have guessed one finger could muster.

"I gave you the beer, Jay," Toby says. "Now go."

"I can stand where I want," Jay says. "You can't tell me not to stand in a public place. Besides, I already finished the beer."

Two other boys—large, but not as tall or thick as Jay—have gathered to watch. The band is now on a break, the smell of fried food not helping Milo's nausea. "You out cruising girls?" one of the boys says to Jay and points to Toby and Milo as the other one laughs.

68

"Are these your new girlfriends?" Jay's sidekicks are both dressed in blue denim shirts and black jeans, the sleeves of their shirts rolled above the elbow revealing tight muscles, thick cords of veins. How is it, Milo wonders, that they've been given the bodies of adults?

Jay takes a pack of matches from his pocket and lights a cigarette then flicks the lit match toward Milo's face, the flame lighting quickly on his cheek before glancing away. Milo feels his pulse quicken, a rabbit readying to run.

"I thought you liked getting lit," Jay says. "I thought you were a flamer just like Tobe."

"Shut the fuck up, Jay," Toby says quietly and Milo understands many things at once: that he's probably *not* the first boy Toby has ever kissed; that Toby is *not* taking summer school for college prep; and that ultimately, there's no such thing as a vacation.

Jay's face calms quickly as he pokes his thick finger into Toby's chest this time. "*You* shut the fuck up."

He bends slightly and whispers in Milo's ear: "Say. You like the same kind of stuff as your man, Tobe?"

Milo pulls away from Jay's breath, sour like the beer he tastes in his own mouth. He wants to move back in time to an hour ago when he's leaning his weight against Toby, who is leaning his weight against the lockers, the cool metal against the palms of Milo's hands. He's never kissed prom royalty before, only Tim, who is clumsy and always sullen afterward, no matter how much pressure he leans against Milo's body at the time, no matter the short, small whimpers of pleasure he echoes when they are actually touching.

Jay looks at his friends then puts his wide hand around the back of Milo's neck, enough to make Milo's knees buckle as he drifts toward the ground. "I know something else you might like," he says.

On his descent Milo looks up in time to see his mother, Bette, elbow her way through the crowd, pushing away one of Jay's sidekicks with the log cabin quilt she has bundled in her arms. "What's going on here?" she says. "What's this? Milo, what are you doing on the ground?"

Jay lets go of Milo's neck and turns to Bette. "He must have fell."

Now everyone seems to be gathered around—Toby, his mother, Ali—and to his side Milo sees his father striding toward him, purposeful steps that Milo knows well. He feels it's best to look at his father this way, off to the periphery as if he is not so much there as a mirage—always arriving, always on the horizon.

Jay leans into Toby and whispers so only he and Milo can hear— "I'll be watching for you, faggot"—then crosses his arms, staying close to the action. Milo's eyes meet his father's and Milo is sure he sees something passing there—disgust? concern?—but it could be the seven beers, or it could be the lightshow that's come on with the ticklish opening cords of "Sweet Home, Alabama," a street-dance favorite.

"What's going on?" Carter demands. "Who's this?"

"My friend, Toby," Milo says and looks at his sandals and his dusty knees. He misses Toby's shiny dress shoes, so shiny he'd be able to see his reflection if he bent close enough to kiss them. He stands up.

"Hi, sir," Toby says. "I'll have to introduce you to my father. He runs the bar here." He's slurring his words slightly but is trying not to sway. "He's a good man to know in town if you like to drink."

"Why would I want to meet your father?" Carter asks, his arms crossed on his chest.

Toby looks confused for a moment then understanding washes over him. "You don't live here."

"Did you tell him we lived here?" Carter asks Milo.

"It doesn't matter," Milo says.

"Ahh," Jay says. "It'll be a long-distance love affair."

"You shut up," Carter says and shakes a finger at Jay, stopping short of touching him. "You don't know a thing about my boy." Milo wants to cry at the ridiculousness of this. As if his own father, in any way, understands him. Five minutes into meeting Jay, he and Milo have a more honest relationship. "Time to go," Carter says and hands Milo the keys.

Milo takes them in his hand and stares at them a moment. "I can't drive."

Carter leans in and smells his breath. "Christ," he says. He looks closer at Milo's mouth, which Milo suspects is bruised. "What have you been doing all night?"

"Nothing."

"Tell me."

Without thinking Milo looks at Toby. "We went to the high school," Milo stammers. "We played in the gym."

"I bet," Jay says, but even his buddies don't laugh as they watch Milo squirm.

"No wonder those guys came harassing you," Carter says.

Milo feels the salty scratch of tears starting in the back of his throat. "I didn't do anything wrong." He looks at Toby's sad face, the brown curls hanging over his eyes, his nose now reddened from the sun and attention. Milo knows what Toby's thinking: tomorrow, I have to face them alone. There is a group of boys at Hellgate High School who haunt the halls looking for Milo on a daily basis during the school year. Even in summer, he doesn't feel safe. Going to the movies, to the mall, to the Big Dipper for a vanilla cone in the afternoon, he is always certain he will see them, coming up in the periphery like his father. He doesn't know how they know about him, or even if they do, but they torment him all the same. His father is close to him now, mere inches away from his face. Milo leans away from his father and puts his lips on Toby's and holds them there, his eyes closed, imagining this moment could be as sweet and innocent as it feels.

Milo breaks the kiss as Carter turns away. He reaches to grab for his father's arm but stumbles and pushes into his shoulder. Without hesitation Carter whips his thick body around, his right arm swinging, and punches his son in the mouth. Milo drops quicker than the hit warrants and crumples to the ground, a hand up to his mouth, which is beginning to swell.

Milo opens his eyes and can see the crowd has parted, blurring Toby, Jay, and his buddies behind him. Toby looks him straight in the face and kicks him once in the side. "Faggot," he says and turns to walk away to join the rest of the crowd. It's the least and most Milo could do. His mother hunkers above him, his father receding behind her. Carter reaches for Milo's arm to help him up, but Bette knocks it away, helping him up herself. She hands him the quilt. "I bought this for you," she says.

Ali emerges from the street with another corn dog in her hand. "What's going on?" she asks Milo. "Where's your friend?"

"Your brother's drunk," Carter says and looks at his son. "Can't you see how hard you're making this on yourself? Can't you see what you're doing?"

"I don't want to be like you."

"Congratulations," Carter says, his voice catching. "You're not even close." He looks around the crowd. "Ali," he says in a rough voice.

"What'd *I* do?" she asks.

"We need you to drive. Your brother's too drunk."

Ali takes the keys, delighted to be driving illegally, no matter the circumstances.

Riding home that night in the back of the minivan, wrapped in his mother's new old quilt, Milo looks longingly out the back window at Corbett, getting smaller and smaller behind them. He thinks of Toby—the softness of his full lower lip, the way he tried, unsuccessfully, to crush a beer can with his long hands before giving up and busting it with his foot. Who's to say he can't come back here, get a job, buy a house, maybe get a fake ID so he can buy Toby some beers. He's seventeen, and looking out the back window of his father's van, he wills himself to remember his whole life is in front of him.

Front and Center

I was in the kitchen cutting iceberg lettuce for the salad bar when Jay came in and told Rigsby the truck had broken down on I-80 and he'd have to leave immediately to pick up the meat. It was already two in the afternoon on New Year's Eve, 1994. This was the busiest night of the year, the one night Jay did a specialty order from Donkersloot Ranch down near North Platte, buying all corn-fed steaks and burgers. Rigs continued wrapping potatoes in pre-cut sheets of tinfoil, placing each potato on the sheet's edge and rolling it a rotation before folding in the sides and securing the ends. He was able to do two at a time, one with each hand. "You may not remember, but you put me on prep work. These potatoes aren't going to wrap themselves."

"Jesus Christ, Rigs," Jay said. "I'm not asking, I'm telling. They're adding our order to a second truck heading to York. Out by the interstate, the truck stop with the big balloon. You meet them there and haul it back." I knew the balloon he was talking about. Earlier that summer my parents had driven me and my brother to South Dakota in a rented camper for what ended up being the worst week of my life. Our first tourist stop had been an hour from home—the water tower painted like a hot air balloon—something we'd driven by a million times before but had never been forced to examine.

"You going to pay me double-time?"

"For doing your job?"

"Wear and tear on the car," Rigs reasoned.

"You know I can't go," Jay said. Rigs calmly wrapped two more potatoes and said that was exactly what he knew. "Fine," Jay said. "Twenty extra bucks." He pointed his cordless phone at Rigs. "But no funny business, you hear me?" He glanced at the cold-prep table where I was standing. "Take her with you. She can babysit. What's your name again?"

"Stephanie," I said and wiped the lettuce bits against my apron as Jay turned back to Rigs. "Or Steph."

Rigs dropped the potatoes. "Come on. My parole officer finds out I'm driving around with an underage girl in my car, I'm liable to end up back in the can." He winked at me.

Jay picked up the phone and started walking back to his office behind the kitchen. "And I want you two back by five, understand me? No funny business."

My parents were the ones who encouraged me to get the job at The Standard, and I use the word "encourage" only because they did. It was, in reality, more of a demand. After the family vacation, they decided that if I wanted to act like an adult they'd start treating me like an adult, so they stopped my allowance and threatened to charge rent. The Standard was the nicer of the two restaurants in our town, the other being a bar on Main Street called the OK Corral, which served premade sandwiches and bags of chips. The Standard had a full menu and bar, along with a senior discount that ran from 4:30 to 6:30 and a Sunday brunch with an omelet bar.

The restaurant itself was classy enough, but the kitchen and wait staff would have given my mom the vapors. Two of the waitresses I worked with had kids without fathers in the picture, and the one waitress who was married told me things about her husband that made it impossible for me to look him in the eye when he dropped her off for her shift. All the women regularly showed up to work hungover, and each night they headed to the OK after work. They always invited me along but I said I had plans; what I didn't have was a fake ID. Fat lot of good it would have done me in Pilgrim, where people I didn't know somehow knew me, stopping me at Pilgrim Foods to ask if I was Rick and Janice's youngest.

The afternoon of New Year's Eve, Rigs had stumbled into work with a wet rag on his head that he periodically rolled like the potatoes, stuffing it each time with fresh ice. Due to some altercation with Jay a few weeks ago, he had found himself on weekdays again, serving a $3.95 roast beef hot shot to divorced and widowed farmers who left a 5-percent tip. Because he had been on better shifts, I hadn't worked with Rigs before, but he was legendary among the wait staff for his partying. At least twice since I'd started, I'd heard he'd been found in the morning passed out in the kitchen, one time supposedly naked. Rigs had been at The Standard over ten years, and the best I could tell, he was somewhere between twenty-eight and forty-five. My best friend, Stacey Blanning, said Rigs had been in jail at some point for dealing and using crystal meth. You couldn't drive ten miles outside of Pilgrim, Nebraska, without hitting an abandoned farmhouse, and according to the local and state papers, we were the meth capital of the world—a title, oddly, that many small towns seemed to vie for. I had a hard time imagining Rigs as a drug dealer. He was shorter than me and wore glasses too large for his face and a moustache underneath that curled down at the ends, yet despite these things he was attractive. If he were to shave or even trim the moustache, invest in a pair of contacts, I wondered if he wouldn't be handsome. Stacey would say I have a tendency to give people too much benefit of the doubt, that maybe if he were to do all these things he wouldn't look any better, with the added disappointment of having tried.

Out in the parking lot, Rigs pointed at a restored El Camino parked by the entrance door, as if I didn't know what car he drove, as if everyone in Pilgrim didn't know that car. The butter-yellow seat rose to meet my legs, and my jeans slid against the soft leather. The dashboard was polished to a shine, the vintage radio gone and replaced with a six-CD player. Rigs slid in next to me, keys in his hand.

"What do you think?" he asked.

"About what?"

He slid the key in the ignition and shook his head. "That's the most I've heard you say at one time, Kelley. I can't tell if you're retarded or just think you're better than me." I hated when people drew attention to how little I spoke, making me even more self-conscious about being shy, but I was thrilled at the use of my last name as my first. There were three other Stephanies in my class of twenty-eight. Rigs tapped the dash to start the CD as he backed out of the parking lot in one smooth move, not looking, it seemed, in the rearview mirror.

The vacation I'd taken the summer before with my parents and my older brother was to the Black Hills. We were to spend seven days looking at rock formations and tracking buffalo and buying ice water at Wall Drug, where we could have our pictures taken with the racist Native American statue outside one of the souvenir shops. On the trip, our folks were cutouts of all the parents we saw—my dad in a cowboy hat without so much as a smudge or crease, my mom in shorts for the first time all summer, her pale, cellulited legs like biscuit dough. Our folks had been planning the vacation for months (*Dances with Wolves* had come out a few years before, and the Badlands were still popular in 1994), and they insisted we continue even after Dad lost his foreman's job at Turner Construction in March, our last hurrah as a family before Peter left for UNL. My mom packed our lunches in a cooler she stored in the rented camper, the white bread soggy because she bought generic sandwich bags that merely folded over instead of the Ziploc bags that closed. We drank Country Time instead of pop and I spent lunches staring longingly at the other families at the local parks, eating their McDonald's at a picnic table. My mother would spread a blanket on the ground, forcing a jovial atmosphere while we ate homemade coleslaw and sandwiches with butter and bologna.

Years later, I'm still horrified to think I complained about these things, although they were the least of my concerns by the end of the week.

Rigs and I drove about forty miles without talking—the stereo blaring Metallica, my eyes on the snow-covered corn and wheat fields. Rigs had a car phone; he was the first person I'd met with one, although five years later they'd be as common as wallets. His was a car phone not a mobile phone and it plugged into his cigarette lighter. Every now and again he would unplug it to light an actual cigarette. He had abandoned the hangover ice towel on his head by now and was drinking Mountain Dew, the bottle nestled between his legs. I was gleeful to think my parents had made me take this job as punishment after the vacation, and yet here I was with a man a decade or two older than me, possibly an ex-con, driving me out of the county. A few miles later, Rigs shouted something at me and I looked at him, my brows drawn in, until he threw his half-smoked cigarette out the window and turned down the music. "I said, we've only got about ten more miles."

I nodded and kept my hands in my lap, hoping he'd turn the music back up, surround us again in the cocoon of not having to talk. We rode a few more miles, the noise still cut, and I wondered if I was supposed to be making conversation. Eventually the silence built up enough in my head I assumed that was the case. "So how long have you worked at The Standard?" I asked.

Rigs reached for his pack of cigarettes on the dash. "He's my uncle," Rigs said. "Jay is."

"Your uncle?"

"It means my mom's brother."

"I know what an uncle is."

"Hard to tell when you repeat it back as a question." I looked out the window and he apologized, said he was hungover and didn't mean to be a dick.

"Does your mom still live around here?"

"She's in Omaha, remarried to a guy with better kids."

77

I thought it was funny that Rigs still thought of himself as a kid, someone tethered to his parents. "Your dad?"

"Dead." I told him I was sorry, and he took a long drag off a new cigarette. "Cancer. My mom used to say I was just like my old man when I was a kid. Who tells that to their child as an insult?"

"What was he like?"

He held up a hand, running it up and down the length of his body. "Pure perfection, if I'm to believe her."

I looked out the window and imagined calling Stacey later that night. I would try to be nonchalant, telling her I'd spent the day with Rigs smoking cigarettes on the way to York. "You know," I'd say, "that guy at the restaurant? The one arrested for drugs a few years back? He's, I don't know, in his late twenties or thirties." Spending the afternoon with Rigs would give me some clout with Stacey, something you shouldn't need with a best friend, but I recognized I did. I thought I would call her later that night but remembered she had a date for New Year's with her new boyfriend who was a senior and complained he wanted her to do more than just suck his dick. I could see the concrete hot air balloon in the distance, just off the interstate, a sign we were getting closer.

"He'd left us by then anyway," Rigs said and I looked at him, confused. "When he died," he explained, "He was two years gone. To us, he was already dead."

I gripped the door handle as we approached the exit ramp at high speed, certain we'd miss it, but Rigs flipped on his blinker at the last possible second and pushed down the brake, easing us to the side.

At the truck stop Rigs called Jay and found out the meat truck had run into some problems an hour east of Kearney, and for now we should sit tight and wait for word. We sidled up to the counter and ordered pie—blueberry for me, coconut meringue for Rigs—along with a Diet Coke and coffee respectively. "How thick is the meringue?" Rigs asked the waitress. "Like this, or this?" He held his pointer finger and thumb an inch than two inches apart. The waitress, an attractive woman with a small waist, took hold of his finger and thumb and maneuvered them to approximately an inch and a half, her hand lingering longer than it needed to. Rigs nodded his approval and handed back our menus.

"Anything over an inch and it's about the show not the taste," Rigs said to me. "The pie's not going to be for shit." He leaned forward, his arms crossed and his face placed in the cavern of his arms. His coffee and my soda came and the waitress lingered a long moment, waiting for Rigs to look up, and when he didn't, she shot me a dirty look, set down the drinks, and left. Rigs sat up and took a hot sip. "Coffee's okay. I'd drink dog urine right now if I thought it would help me feel better."

"Hangover's are the worst," I said, and Rigs turned to me, amused.

"You know about hangovers?"

I shrugged. "I got shit-faced on vacation last summer. It was pretty awful."

"Who'd you go on vacation with?"

He had me. "My parents. They're totally lame. My brother and I snuck out one night and found a pretty cool party at the other end of the campsite. My dad ended up busting it down." I leaned forward to take a sip of my Diet Coke through the straw, then thought better of it and lifted my glass. Lifting the glass seemed more mature, but I wondered if Rigs would think I looked sexy drinking from the straw. I pushed the glass away, no longer thirsty.

"You're what? Fifteen? Sixteen? Fourteen? Of course you went on vacation with your parents. Of course they're lame."

Peter and I had snuck out of the camper when our folks fell asleep—Peter, a popular kid who partied every weekend, swiped our dad's whiskey—and we stumbled upon four college guys traveling on their way to Manitoba from Kansas. Peter let them see the bottle and they called us over, motioning to the cooler of beer. I hadn't drunk before that night and I was still on my first Coors when my father found us, his bald head shiny in the moonlight.

One of the guys had his hand on my back, rubbing circles under my shirt. I had wanted so badly for something to happen, but when it appeared that was a possibility, I was petrified—relieved to the point of tears when my dad showed up, although I played it like I was angry, embarrassed to be led home.

The next day our parents woke us at 7:00 a.m. sharp and told us to gear up for a day of South Dakota fun, assuming we were hungover, which Peter was. While my father and Pete were showering, my mother sat on the picnic table outside our camper, her feet on the bench, and handed me a cup of coffee. I took a sip of the bitter drink and thought this was the beginning of my punishment, but as it settled into my stomach, a swirling warmth and energy, I took it for the gift it was. I didn't know if my father had told her he'd seen me sitting with the college boy, but I had recategorized nothing happening into a colossal disappointment.

"It was no big deal," I said, but my mother waved her hand to indicate she didn't want me to go on and pointed to a cornfield on the horizon. There was a rusted grouping of abandoned farm equipment in the field and behind that, hardly visible, a deer. The deer bent down and investigated the dirt. There was a noise somewhere that I couldn't hear and the deer took off in a shot, her delicate hooves hardly seeming to touch the earth.

"I was young once, too, you know," my mother said, and it took me a moment to realize she was referring to me, not the deer.

"Dad's going to blow this out of proportion," I said, and a year ago he would have, but he had become unpredictable since losing his job months before. "We just had a couple of beers," I said. "It's not a crime, you know."

"It is too."

"Technically, but you know what I mean."

"You need to be more responsible, Stephanie. Make better decisions. I need to be able to trust you." What she meant was she needed to not have to worry about me; she had enough of that with my father and Peter.

I scooted my butt off the picnic table and told my mother I was going to shower. "Enjoy the spa while you can," she said. "Your dad and I have quite a day planned for you two." The spa was four communal showerheads with no hot water and a blurry mirror made of fake glass. Our folks had planned a six-mile hike and a late morning at Mount Rushmore, another shitty picnic on our worn wool blanket. But I didn't complain—I didn't complain once— and somehow this made it worse, my father finally throwing his soggy sandwich back in the cooler and telling us it was time for a restaurant. In the Golden Nugget the air-conditioning was cranked unreasonably high, and I found myself shivering in my sweaty clothes. We ordered off what my dad called "the right side of the menu"—the expensive dinner side. "Happy vacation," he said, drinking a whiskey and Coke in the middle of the day. "Happy family time." Our lunches came and the portions were huge—a steak for my father the size of the plate. We all ended up leaving over half of what we'd ordered, but even so, Dad insisted we each get dessert.

Rigs came back from the restroom and set a piece of paper on the counter. "The waitress. She gave me her number."

I took another bite of my pie, conscious now I should have ordered something that wouldn't stain my teeth. "Are you going to call her? You could call her from your car. That would impress her."

He snorted. "My old man left me that car. That's my inheritance."

"It's a cool car." In the last twenty years it had gone from being a joke to a classic, and a decade later, driving down the interstate, I'd see one and wonder if Rigs had held onto his.

"She's not my type," he said, and I looked at the waitress as she bent over the counter to take a man's order, the jeans she was wearing a size too small and suggestive. He pushed his pie away, half eaten. "I called Jay for an update when I hit the can. They got a mechanic to look at the truck—it's something with the radiator. Nothing they're going to fix by tonight. Some other dude is going to load up another truck and we're supposed to head north on 81 and meet them." He looked at me and laughed. "Meat them? Get it?" I laughed because Rigs expected me to, but honestly, the joke was pretty dumb.

We drove for another hour or so north of York to a small town with a population of four hundred. The town appeared deserted, only two girls around my age walking down the snowy sidewalk on Center Avenue. I recognized the boots one girl was wearing, the same pair of yellow goulashes I had worn the year before and that I'd be wearing again this year, our Christmas the leanest it'd been in years.

Rigs got a call on his car phone and answered with one hand, the other on the wheel. "Rigs, here." He listened for a bit, and I tried to play it cool—a phone, in the car! "That's bullshit," he said. "You told us the truck was on its way." He paused and I watched the girls turn off Center onto 5th. I wondered if they, unlike me, had plans for New Year's Eve. Stacey was out with Brandon, and Peter was with his friends. Even my folks were heading down to The Standard to dance their middle-aged dances and watch the ball drop on 1994.

"You want us to just come *back*?" Rigs asked, his voice angry then contorting into a laugh. "Jesus Christ, Uncle Jay. Where's your can-do attitude." He shook his head as Jay's voice wah-wahhed through the phone. "I don't think so," he said. "You wanted me to pick up the meat, then I'm going to pick up the meat." I heard Jay's voice, angry now like Rig's. "I guess you should have sent someone else then," Rigs said. "Someone who can stay out of trouble," and Jay said something back although I couldn't make out the words. Rigs nodded along, his face tight like he was straining to hear although Jay was yelling in his ear. "I guess that's on your head," Rigs said and hung up the phone.

He gunned the gas and pulled back on the road, turning on 5th toward a convenience store we'd passed as we drove into town. He pulled in the parking lot and turned off the engine, his eyes pointed through the windshield. "Come in or wait in the car?"

Inside, he headed to the back cooler and grabbed a twelve-pack of Busch Light, the same brand my father drank. "What're you doing?" I asked.

He stopped, and looked at the beer in his hand. "I believe I'm about to purchase an alcoholic beverage."

I stood there stupidly before following him to the register. He set the beer on the counter and pulled out his worn leather wallet, asking the clerk for two packs of Camel Lights and where the high school was. The boy—my age, or a year or two older—didn't even card him. I took a step closer to Rigs.

"So, what'd Jay say?" I asked when we got back in the El Camino.

"You know what I get paid?" he said. "A buck over minimum wage, and that fucker is my uncle. My mom's goddamn brother. I'm not chasing some fucking meat all over the state."

It was four in the afternoon by now. The dinner crowd would come in late tonight Rigs had said, the restaurant filling at eight instead of six. The kitchen would stay open a few extra hours to gear up for New Year's and close at eleven o'clock so Rigs could hang up his apron and come around to the bar side, sit down, and have a beer and a shot with the crowd. Everyone was generous on New Year's Eve, he said. Everyone. Most of the customers would say it was the best goddamn steak they'd ever eaten and leave a ten-dollar tip, because there was hope at this point of a new year beginning. My father, who had started at Turner as a grunt, was unemployed for the first time since he'd turned sixteen, and even he would be down there, my mother in the same blouse she'd worn the New Year's before.

In front of the school, Rigs put the car in neutral and pulled on the parking brake. He popped the tab on one of the beers and passed it to me, then opened a second for himself. I took a small sip, keeping my gag reflex in check. "I don't usually drink beer," I said, and he looked at me, amused again. Across the street, two boys in letterman jackets were shooting hoops without a net on the basket, the metallic clang from each missed shot audible inside the car. "How come you brought us to the school?" I asked, and he said it was a good place to drink since school was out; no cops would have a reason to come by. "Who knows," he said. "Maybe some more folks will show up and we'll have us a party." We listened to the Metallica CD then moved on to Megadeth. Already the sun was beginning to edge toward the horizon, the sky tamping down with the threat of more snow. At best, we'd make it back to Pilgrim by 6:30.

After another beer, Rigs pointed his can toward the windshield where the two girls from earlier were heading to the guys on the basketball court. "See." He got out of the car and swooped the twelve-pack up from the back and tucked it in his arm like a newborn. I followed behind.

"You guys here to party?" he asked and I saw the girls look to each other.

"Depends," one of the boys said. "Can you buy?"

"Can you pay?" Rigs said, and they bartered a deal that Rigs could drink his cut from a case, so Rigs and I got back in the car and headed to the convenience store where I waited in the car this time. He came out with the beer and threw it in the bed of his El Camino—the fridge he'd called it earlier—and we went back to the courts. The game was in full swing by now, both of the girls on defense and the boys shooting over their heads. The boy who'd asked for the beer earlier—Tony—said his folks were in North Platte for the night and we could party at his house if we wanted, so the two guys climbed in the bed of the car followed by one of the girls, but Rigs stopped the last one, the one in my goulashes. "Here," he said. "No use you messing up that pretty hair," and he ran a hand down the back of her skull, giving her a pat on the butt as she climbed in the car. Her name was Dana and I instantly didn't like her. On the way to Tony's, Rigs called Jay to give him Tony's number in case he needed to get a hold of us. He repeated it twice, and I could hear Jay yelling that if we weren't out looking for the goddamned truck, we'd better come the fuck back and stop at a grocery on the way. Rigs pointed out he didn't have any money—"That's what you get for not trusting me with the petty cash anymore"—and told Jay to call Tony's when the meat reached town, and that he swore we'd drop everything to take care of it. Jay was still yelling as Rigs hung up, and even I knew the only reason Rigs had called was to impress Dana with the phone.

By my third beer at Tony's we'd started a game of quarters, an impossible game I couldn't have accomplished sober although I knew that wasn't the point. The more I missed, the more I drank, a setup that made me happy. I thought of what Stacey would say the next day, calling to tell me about her date with Brandon. Maybe I'd tell her I was too hungover to talk, and I'd have to call her back. Then maybe I'd wait a day or two to let her wonder. Tony and Alyssa—the other girl—had abandoned the game already and were making out in front of the TV while Rigs continued to win round after round. Six or so beers in and he could close one eye and bounce the quarter in at any angle. "How do you keep hitting that shit, man?" Scot asked, and Rigs got up and stood behind Dana, smoothing a hand down her arm from her elbow to her thumb. "It's all in the wrist," Rigs said, and he shadowed Dana's hand for the release. Sure enough, it went in.

"What about me?" I said, and Rigs raised his eyebrows to me with his wry, amused grin.

"You ready to play, Kelley?" he asked, and I nodded, unsure exactly what I'd consented to. "All right then," he said, and moved behind me.

He put his hand on mine, the quarter tight in my grip. "Like this," he said as Dana glared at me, and he moved his hand up and down, slowly but rhythmically, as I felt my face grow warm. Despite the roughness of his palm and fingers, I felt like my hand was being guided by water. He bent his mouth to my ear, his voice dropping a decibel. "How's that feel, Kelley?"

I pushed back my chair nearly toppling Rigs in the process, and he held up his hands as if to say, "no harm, no foul," a smile on his face.

"I have to go to the bathroom," I announced, my face still burning.

On the toilet, I let my head drop between my knees, my stomach swirling, the taste of metal in my mouth. The bathroom was decorated much like my parents' with outdated linoleum and seashells on the counter. I could imagine my mother at home putting on her makeup, my dad precounting out drinks by the dollars in his wallet. It was seven o'clock on New Year's Eve, and standing up to button my pants, all I could think was that I didn't want to be here and what a loser I was for feeling that way.

I came out of the bathroom and into the kitchen and saw Rigs had Dana pushed against the fridge as they kissed each other, his hand under her shirt exposing the winter-white flab of her belly. I stood a long moment watching their elastic mouths push together, wondering what they'd done with all their teeth. In the living room, I sat down, aware of a slow headache starting in the back of my skull. Scot peered over the arm of the La-Z-Boy where he'd retreated and said, "Hey. You want another beer?"

I thought for a moment. "No thanks," I said, and only then did I realize he'd asked because he wanted me to get one for him.

I spent the next two hours on the couch flipping magazines—Tony's mother's *Good Housekeeping* and his father's *Time*. There was an article in *Time* about the acquittal of Lorena Bobbitt and another about whether Tonya Harding would be named to the Olympic team. Tony and Alyssa had left by this point, and Scot sat in the La-Z-Boy smoking cigarettes even though Tony had asked us not to. At one point the ash dropped on the armrest burning a small hole, and a few minutes later when Scot noticed, he swept the ash on the floor. I was tired and bored. Looking at the grandfather clock—where someone, for god knows what reason, had cracked an egg—I saw at best we'd make it home by ten, an hour before the kitchen was to close, but what was even the point if we didn't have the meat? We never heard from Jay or the distributor, and it no longer seemed worth it to spend these hours wasting time just to have a story to mock up for Stacey, something to make me feel cool when I knew the truth. 1995. This year I'd turn seventeen, and in the fall I'd be a senior.

Embarrassed as I was, I headed down the hallway and knocked on the door. "Rigs?" I said. "You in there?" I heard a rustling noise and then he answered the door with his shirt off. I tried to keep my eyes on his face instead of his chest, concentrating on the reddened whites of his eyes and his dilated pupils. "You ready?" I asked, and Rigs ducked back in and grabbed his shirt, said he'd only be a second. On the dresser were small squares of tinfoil with burn marks in the middle, and I wondered if Rigs had taken them from the potatoes earlier, why he would do such a thing, and then I realized that of course they were too small for that.

A few minutes later he met me in the kitchen. I asked Rigs if he was okay to drive and he said he'd be fine, grabbing a beer for the road. He lit a cigarette and threw the match on the floor where it burned a small, black spot into the linoleum. Empty cans littered the counter tops, and the four coffee mugs we'd used for quarters were still on the table next to the carcass of a half-eaten chicken we'd found in the fridge and two empty bags of chips. From the back bedroom wafted the smell of burnt plastic and air freshener. Dana came out. Her hair was messed up, but other than that, she looked the same. I'm not quite sure what I had expected. "So you'll call me?" she said to Rigs, and he said of course he would and patted the front pocket of the shirt he'd put back on.

"You forgot it," Dana said and held out a piece of paper.

He folded it into his pants pocket and gave her a chaste kiss on the cheek. Rigs picked up my coat and handed it to me, then put on his own. "Time to hit the road." As we were leaving, I saw the phone on the wall, the receiver on the floor. It had been off the hook the whole time.

We drove past the concrete balloon—large and looming but now invisible in the night, more felt than seen, like a hand fluttering past your head in the dark. It began to snow, a light dusting of flakes that rushed toward the windshield like blurry white dots, heading into warp speed in a science-fiction movie.

"Why'd you pick Dana?" I asked. I felt relieved yet rejected that this had happened, unsure if I'd had any interest in Rigs at all.

He glanced my way. "You ever heard the phrase, 'don't shit where you eat?'"

"No."

"Well that's why."

I thought about this a moment. "Am I where you shit or where you eat?"

Rigs lit another cigarette. "I guess it doesn't matter, you just can't be both." In my classes at school, teachers liked to talk about all the steps taken for women in the last few decades—female astronauts, female doctors, even a first female Nebraska governor—but somehow we were still defined by men: where they shat and where they ate.

As we pulled into The Standard an hour and a half later, Rigs found a spot out front. The parking lot was full except where Rigs had pulled in, and I could see that to the side of the restaurant even the overflow lot was to capacity. Rigs was that kind of lucky: a front-spot kind of guy, driving his father's legacy.

"You think we're going to get in trouble?" I asked and Rigs shook his head, pulling out the last cigarette from the two packs he'd bought earlier in the day.

"Jay'll have his ass in a bunch for a week or two, but he'll get over it. We're already on dayshift. Not like it can get much worse than being stiffed by a bunch of farmers over breakfast." Inside I could see the party was in full swing, Jay by the hostess stand with a beer in his hand and a plastic crown on his head that read *1995*. Rigs tapped the cigarette on the dash before lighting it. "Just go home," he said. "I'll deal with my uncle."

Maybe Rigs was right. In a few weeks, it would be like this day never happened.

I got home around eleven o'clock, an hour before the new year would begin. Not surprisingly, my mom was still up and waiting for me in the kitchen, an open Busch Light on the table, her fingers swollen from twisting her rings.

"I don't even know where to start with you, Stephanie Elizabeth," she said. "It didn't occur to you to call me? It didn't occur to you I might be worried to death?"

I sat in the chair, amazingly tired, without enough energy to take off my coat. "You were the one who wanted me to take this job."

"Oh, that's rich," she said. "This one's my fault too. I called Jay at The Standard and he said he sent you off with that Rigs fellow, and I asked him what he was thinking letting a sixteen-year-old loose with that man." She looked at me. "He didn't even realize you were a child."

I perked up. "He thought I was eighteen?"

She rubbed a hand over her face, her skin pulling like rubber. "Don't go missing the point on me here. You could have been hurt. You could have been murdered."

"Nothing happened," I said. It was becoming the story of my very young life.

She looked at me, her age etched on her face. "Your father and I have been looking forward to this night for months," she said. "Not that that's the point, but how could it not occur to you to call me? Pete goes away to college and I don't hear from him for months, but you I at least expect to call."

She opened her mouth to say more, but I cut her off with an "I'm sorry," and the apology seemed to take the wind out of her sails. She went to the fridge and pulled the door open, asking if I was hungry. I told her I could eat, realizing that, other than a handful of chips, I hadn't eaten since the truck-stop pie.

She set a lasagna in front of me with one row missing—three pieces for her, Dad, and Peter—Pete home from his first semester and already on academic probation. "You need to think about your actions," she said, carving another row with a butcher knife. "Do you have any idea how worried I was about you? Anything could have happened to you. Anything." Once when I was a child, I had a bee sting me on the inside of my eyelid—what the doctor called a million in one shot. Since then, my mother has thought I was special, although special in her worst-case-scenario mind often looked like cursed.

"We just drove around," I said and grabbed the milk from the fridge. There was a near-empty twelve-pack of beer on the shelf. "Where's Dad?"

"He went down to The Standard to wait for you." The microwave dinged and she grabbed a fork from the drawer then shut it with her hip.

"Rigs went inside, so Dad should know by now that I'm home."

"He should, shouldn't he?" She sat down and took a bite of the lasagna before scooting over the plate. "That's good," she said and cut another piece, putting it in the microwave.

"Maybe you could go down and meet him. Still salvage the night."

"Your father?" she said. "Being out of a job has been hard on him, but he's not the only one. You think I like making my own laundry detergent or never eating out? I went to North Platte last week and looked into food stamps."

"We went to a party," I said. "We were supposed to meet the truck but Rigs blew it off, and we ended up at some guy's house playing quarters, and then Rigs had sex with some girl. They might have been doing drugs, I don't know."

She put down her fork and picked up my hand. "Are you okay? Are you sure?"

I shrugged. "I was mainly bored. None of the boys even looked at me."

"Oh, sweetie," she said and squeezed my hand. "Don't try to grow up so fast. You have plenty of time for men to disappoint you."

We sat for a long time at the table, eating our lasagna, until she stood to put her plate on the counter, giving my shoulder another squeeze as she walked by. "We'll talk about all this in the morning. You get to bed. We'll figure out a punishment tomorrow."

"A punishment?" I said, incredulous. "You're the one who made me get a job. I *had* to go!"

"Fine. We'll discuss your job performance tomorrow. However you want to put it. Your father's going to get an earful when he gets home," she said, although I knew she'd never tell him what had happened.

I started down the hallway and heard her call after me to not forget to wash my face. Stupid face, I thought. I stopped in the bathroom and did as she said, my features in sharp focus. After my father took us to the restaurant on vacation, we stopped sleeping in the camper and got a room at the Holiday Inn. We ate steak dinners the next two nights, and he bought tacky souvenirs of stuffed buffalos and snow globes for me and Peter—gifts we threw away a few months later. He bought a Black Hills gold necklace for my mother and stood behind her as he clasped it, her jaw clenched. Back home, we returned to white-bread lunches with butter and bologna, five-dollar dinners in the Crock-Pot. "Why'd he do that?" I asked my mother a few weeks after the vacation, and she shook her head and said, "Because men get the right to misbehave." I thought about the waitresses I worked with—the two single mothers bitching about their missing child support and the wife, the one they all envied, with a crescent of yellow bruise always present on her face. Dana would spend the next week waiting for a call that wouldn't come, and Tony's mom would return from her New Year's celebration to find her house in ruins, a permanent cigarette burn on the armrest of her chair, egg yolk dried in the wood grain of her clock.

In bed, I lay on my back with the room spinning around me, the lasagna in my stomach a solid thing holding me to the earth. I thought about the hot air balloon: held to the ground, heavy and immobile. The snow had stopped falling and the moon was bright, so much so I could hold my hand out in front of me and see every line, every freckle that hadn't faded since summer. My mother was the one who told me I'd have to get a job, and I realized now it wasn't about the punishment, but that they were cutting corners—my allowance an unnecessary expense. My father should have come home by now, but I guessed he was bellied up to the bar, not a care in the world, waiting to see what the night would bring. Such optimism on New Year's Eve, Rigs had said, such generosity. For all I knew my father believed it, the future as shiny as Rigs's El Camino, gleaming front and center in the parking lot.

I heard a scattering of noise out my window, a muffled cheer, and knew it had just passed midnight. All around town—all around the world—men were celebrating the good fortune of 1995. "Here's to it," my father might say to Rigs, clanking their glasses together. "Here's to the next best year of our lives." And on the other side of the wall I knew my mother was in the kitchen, our empty plates rinsed and nestled in the dishwasher, her hands folded in her lap as she twisted her rings, as she waited for her husband to come home.

A Possible Story

He holds out his hand and says, "Pam," and she wonders for just a moment if maybe he does recognize her, but it's not that. He knows her name because they've been corresponding the past few days about his visit. The directions, where to park, what time he should plan on arriving.

"Hello," she says. "My class is anxious to meet you. They really loved your latest book." Pam has no idea whether they loved his book or not, or even read it, but she knows from her own trips as a visiting writer that it's a nice lie to hear.

"Thank you, thanks so much." He smiles warmly and drops her hand as he adjusts the strap on his book bag, a mahogany leather satchel worn smooth from his hip. He's older than she remembers, as if he's aged in double-time to how she's changed in the past eight years.

Her colleague from the English Department comes up behind her and holds out his hand. "Floyd Josselson. Nice to meet you."

"You too, Floyd. Rex Enger." Pam wondered how he'd introduce himself. If he'd use the middle initial like he does for publication or just the first and last name. Details like this she can't remember. Rex adjusts the perfect book bag higher on his shoulder and showers them both with a smile. "I'm honored you guys had me down."

Pam joined the faculty at Deridan College that fall, and at the first department meeting it was obvious that as the new fiction writer she should join the Visiting Writers Committee. The committee planned the fall schedule the previous spring—contacted the writers, set the fees—and when she got the list in her new faculty mailbox, his name—Rex T. Enger—solidified on the page while the others receded. He was coming fall semester, and there was nothing she could do about it.

Eight years ago when she was passionate about writing—passionate in a way only a beginning writer in her twenties can be—she took a week-long noncredit workshop from Rex T. Enger and slept with him. It was before she went to graduate school, before she published a thing. Before she even knew that other students had slept with writing professors. That week she was quiet in workshops although she longed to talk. She knew even as an amateur that her writing was better than the other students. Rex didn't seem to agree, or at least didn't single her out in class as anything extraordinary, but on the fourth night of class he invited her back to his upgraded faculty hotel room for a drink after the class happy hour—their one social outing with the professor that she understood now was included in his fee. He said it would be a chance to talk one-on-one about her writing.

It was the only night in her life she drank bourbon. Later, when it was clear it was a night for recklessness, she poured some between her legs and pushed his head down, no matter some soaked through the sheets and into the mattress. It wasn't her bed. Eight years later, she still can't remember such details without blushing or a flicker of pride. She returned home knowing it was a fling and she'd never see him again, but satisfied she finally understood what it meant to be a writer, to be careless and wild and uninhibited. What did she have to feel guilty about? After all, he was the married one, not her, and it wasn't like the class was for a grade. She never forgot though how the next awkward morning she teased him by dancing her fingers under the covers and asking what grade he would give her. He responded, "B-plus." Whether that was for her lovemaking or her writing, she didn't know.

Shortly after the workshop she applied to graduate school, and it was a few years—maybe three—before she realized what a joke that night had been. How fraught with clichés. But now that was eight years in the past. Eight years! She finished her master's and a PhD and, toward the end of her program, published a short-story collection to lukewarm success, enough to get her a good job at a decent school with a reasonable class load. She uprooted her family—her husband, Josh, and their daughter, Lou—and moved twelve-hundred miles to a small liberal arts college in Colorado, not two hours from her only one-night stand, who now, eight years later, was visiting her school. A thousand dollars for a class visit, a reading, and a free dinner, and then he'd be on his way home, those stupidly optimistic and promiscuous days still buried, her professional demeanor intact. The last thing she wanted was her new colleagues thinking she was a sexual liability, a loose cannon with no sense of boundaries. She'd never been so glad to be forgettable in the sack.

Floyd puts a hand on Pam's shoulder and turns back to Rex. "I see you've met our rising star, Dr. Langton."

Pam cringes. She wants people to say things like this but not in front of her, and not in front of someone with seven books—all from Knopf—while hers is a small press out of the southwest.

Rex takes her book from his worn satchel along with a pen. "Will you sign it?" It's a nice gesture, just the type of thing Pam expects from someone with his savvy and reputation.

"I'd love to, thanks." She stares at the book, now in her hands. Does he really not know who she is?

He looks at her awkwardly and holds out the pen a little further, his hands papery like her parents'.

"I'm sorry," she fumbles. "I never know what to write." Now

that she's said that, she realizes she can't merely sign her name, there needs to be a note of some kind. She blushes and feels her underarms begin to sweat. "I'll just put it aside," she says and Rex nods, smiling.

"Don't forget to return it."

"Oh, no," she says. "I won't forget." She stares at him a moment longer than is comfortable for either of them, then turns away and looks at the filling room.

They scheduled the reading during her evening class to guarantee an audience, and it's only because they're required to be here that her students have shown up. She asked them to come with two questions prepared for the Q&A with Rex; she threatened to grade them on this. One thing she hadn't expected when she started teaching was apathy from her creative-writing students. As an undergraduate her writing classes were a portal to something and someone else, a world she hadn't imagined lived inside of her. It was like falling in love for the first time. She'd spend hours and days and weeks working on her stories, only to see the other students come in with stories they finished that morning, unstapled and well below the page limit. Now as a teacher she tries to put herself in their shoes, to remember how she felt about her other classes like biology and pre-calc, but it's unimaginable to her that they don't care about writing, yet are so interested in being writers.

She glances over at Rex and can remember so clearly being in the bathroom of his hotel room shortly after he announced that he would like to see her in her underwear. She looked at her blurry image wobbling in the hotel mirror and thought, this is an opportunity that doesn't present itself everyday. She was embarrassed by her matronly undergarments and the smell of her own skin, but none of that mattered in the face of adventure, in the face of a possible story. Sometimes now the only adventure she has is wrestling a three-year-old into the grocery cart. Try writing a story about that.

Pam checks her watch again—a nervous habit—and tells Rex they'll be starting in two minutes. He coughs and she asks if he'd like some water, then hands him the bottle she packed for herself in her bag.

"So this is your first year here?" he asks.

"It is, I just started in the fall."

"And before that?"

"I was working on my PhD at Western Michigan." When he knew her, she was a secretary in Minneapolis; this won't ring any bells.

"And how do you like Colorado?" As she answers she wonders if he's as bored with her answers as she is with his questions. She doesn't remember much of their conversation from that night eight years ago, other than it must have been embarrassing. Her sitting in one of those uncomfortable nondescript hotel chairs, him stretched out on the bed, answering where he got his ideas and explaining how exciting it was to be in the *New Yorker* the first time, but how now it was kind of blasé. One of her students, Sondra—a writer whose work is undisciplined and rambling—comes over to ask Rex if he'll answer a question. "I'm too shy to ask in front of everyone else. Dr. Langton can tell you, I'm a real shy girl." Pam would never have thought such a thing and knows that Sondra's slipping into the role she thinks this man wants her to play, just like she does with the male students in her small group.

Rex folds his arms across his chest and leans in intently. "Yes?"

"Do you think it's important to wait for inspiration to strike or to write every day?" Rex, god bless him, nods his head as if he's thinking, as if he hasn't been asked this same question for the last thirty years. He answers and Sondra smiles extensively. "I agree," she says. "I keep telling myself that no matter how tired I am, I've got to drag ass out of bed every morning and do it."

"And do you?" Rex asks.

Sondra cocks her head to the side and giggles like the shy girl she's not. "Sometimes."

Rex mingles with Pam's students and colleagues, the few people from the community who have come. She curses her decision to wear a white blouse that shows sweat stains, shows her nerves as clearly as if she's wearing a sign. She turns to Rex. "Anything else you need before we get started?"

"I'm good."

As the newest member of the committee she's been asked to introduce his reading, one of many steps she'll have to climb on her ascent toward tenure. This is the second reading they've hosted since she came to Deridan, and she remembers the awkward introduction at the first one. Charles Grealy, a tenured medievalist, had rested his thin, clumsy body on the podium and said, "Well, you've all seen the flier for Liz Vander's visit," trailing off with a head nod toward the writer and her book. Liz sat there an uncomfortable moment staring back at Charles before realizing the introduction was over and it was time for her to read.

At six thirty Pam walks to the podium at the front of the small, well-lit room and the noise dies down. She smiles and pulls the typed introduction from her pocket. It includes the names of his books and how long he's been in his teaching position, along with quotes and reviews saying he is the rightful heir to Fitzgerald's throne, the American Chekhov, and other embarrassing things critics have said, all most likely his friends. She now knows from the glowing blurbs on the back of her own book that that's how these things work. She's begun to doubt whether anyone is ever really reading anyone new. Has anyone she's not related to bought a copy of the book? And did she really think that book would change her? She steps down from the podium to polite applause and Rex takes the stage with a hardback copy of his book and slips on a pair of reading glasses, his eyes owly behind the thick lenses.

He reads an older story, one she read herself years ago when she admired his writing. She still does, she supposes, but not in the same way. His stories feel more self-indulgent now, when before they seemed difficult in a way that made her stupid and him smart. She looks out at her students and the few other people in the audience. They are rifling quietly in book bags and purses, their eyes creeping shut. A man she doesn't recognize puts a pencil eraser up his nose, closes his mouth, then breathes out quickly and huffs it into his hand. Her first reading after her book came out had an audience of six, including her mother and two of her friends. Her mother, mercifully, bought yet another copy.

Rex snaps the book shut when he finishes, startling the audience into a smattering of applause. She wonders if this is why he brought the hardback volume. Will she ever know all these tricks? Will she ever need to?

She walks back to the podium with a smile and thanks Rex then turns to the audience and asks if there are any questions. They stare at her. Sondra, the supposedly shy girl who is dedicated to her writing, pushes buttons on her cell phone. Scott, a boy who shows promise, scribbles on his notepad, while Rae, a girl who is present only because she's used all her absences and doesn't want to get kicked out of her sorority, lolls a mint around in her mouth. Floyd raises his hand. "Yes?" she says, and points to him so he can ask Rex if he writes every day. Pam can remember not too long ago how wonderful it was to go to readings, to have someone tell her a story they had made up themselves, the world full of infinite adventures. She remembers Rex walking into the workshop eight years ago with a confident gait and all the right answers, how exciting it was to think in one mere week she'd be a better writer.

They limp through a few more questions, and toward the end of the hour Rex deftly steers the conversation to his time as a brewery worker when he was a kid, something college students are interested in and a story she's certain he's told a hundred times. She remembers reading an essay he wrote about it and published in *Ploughshares*.

Afterward, she leaves Rex trapped with Floyd Josselson, a too-loud talker who has a friend in common in Boulder.

In the bathroom, washing her hands, Pam begins to tremble. She's relieved that Rex has forgotten her, but she hadn't expected there would be not even a flicker of recognition. She didn't tell her husband she'd be seeing Rex today or even about the night eight years ago that they shared. Rather than being jealous, she was worried he'd look at her with an accusatory glance as if to ask, whatever happened to *that* girl. Scrubbing Lou in the tub or dog vomit from the carpet or pots after she burns another meal, wouldn't she like to know the answer to that question too.

After the reading, she drives Rex and Floyd to the mediocre Italian restaurant across the street. It's either that or a Thai buffet, which seems too cheap even if the food is better. She still has her unsigned book in her book bag, a stupid "Best Wishes!" on the tip of her pen. Originally she thought the worse thing would be to be caught alone with Rex, with one other person the second worst. What if the third wheel was able to detect the sexual tension? The dormant affair from years ago? Fat chance of that now, she thinks, as Rex pops an Altoid in his mouth and surveys the menu. "Is the clam sauce any good here?" he asks, and she wants to smack the menu from his hand.

As they wait for their food, Rex asks about her teaching load, how her book has been received, how she describes her students. She doubts he cares enough to make her feel bad about herself but it feels like that's what he's doing. Her course load is too high, her students not as good as his, her shitty little book not even sniffed at by Knopf. Is she really this jealous of a person? And if she dislikes him so much, why does she care if he remembers her? Because it's apparent to Pam now that she does care. She tucks her hair behind her ears so it looks short like when she met him. When Rex asks her between bites of his eggplant parmesan if she has any children, she tells him yes, a three-year-old girl, then asks about his two sons, now grown and out of college. Part of his shtick all those years ago had been that he was a good father, even a good husband, which infuriates her all the more. He looks surprised she knows about his children and she leans forward, seizing her opening.

"I took a class from you. A week-long summer course in New York." It had cost her most of a semester's student loan.

Rex smiles at her, his big seven-book grin expanding. "You're one of my success stories," he says and she looks hard at his face, the lines and wrinkles cut deeper near his eyes when he smiles. "Of course," he continues. "I remember you now."

She shakes her head. "I don't think you do."

He apologizes and admits she's right, something she doubts he admits very often. Eight years ago he lounged on the hotel bed with one foot curled on top of the other, telling her about the stories he'd published. Did she know the first one he sent out was accepted? And that he's only been rejected a handful of times? *Why did he feel the need to tell her this?* He played to her sensibilities of what it meant to be a writer and she never would have guessed all those years ago the sacrifice in front of her: the lost boyfriends, the fights with her brother over autobiographical material, the rows she'd have with Josh over her time-consuming "hobby." Rex had made it look so easy—seven books published while he left his family at home to go off and have affairs. She's angry suddenly, because it's nothing like that. And she's angry because he stands for everything she's given up by getting married and becoming an academic, when what she wanted was to be a writer. She knows even at thirty-six she's never going to be anything special. She'll continue to publish stories and a book every five or so years, but none of it will matter. Teaching is a *job*; writing is a *job*. And how long had she known this? Pam's heart pounds in her chest but she can't find the words. She doesn't even know what it is she wants to say.

Floyd switches the conversation to the Broncos—a Colorado standard, even for academics—and this moves naturally to skiing and, finally, Boulder politics. At the end of the meal, when the waitress asks if they'd like dessert, Rex orders a third glass of wine and drinks it quickly, a slight shake in his hands as he brings the glass to his mouth. Maybe this is why he reads from a hardback book, she thinks, so the shaking is less evident. Rex makes no motion to pick up the check, assuming it's covered by the university, but only two of the meals will be—the visiting writer and one host—and none of the alcohol. On Monday, she'll find an envelope in her mailbox from Floyd for his portion of the bill, a tip for fifteen percent figured down to the penny. She drives Floyd to his car first, courting now a moment alone with Rex, imagining what she will say. Floyd climbs out and shakes Rex's hand through the window, then fumbles for his keys as he unlocks one of the beat-up Hondas in the faculty lot.

"It's nice here," Rex says, as she pulls away, heading toward the visitor parking lot. She assumes he means the weather, the first bite of winter as the sun goes down. "A little cooler than we get down in Boulder." It's a comment that could have been made to anyone, the idle chitchat of polite strangers. Why did he need to tell her about his success all those years ago? About all his stories in the *New Yorker*? Just whom was he trying to convince?

At his SUV, Rex reaches in his perfect bag and pulls out a pair of glasses, different from the ones he wore at the reading. "For driving," he explains. "I get black spots in my vision. I shouldn't drive at night." She looks at his face. He's in that decade now when her own parents started the great decline, her father no longer going to McDonald's every morning for a coffee and paper as he had for years before heading to work. He slipped six months ago and it left him much worse than injured: scared. "I remember when I started teaching," Rex says, "I thought I'd never forget a student. I can still tell you the full names of every student I taught my first year, but now I can't remember the kids from last semester."

She thinks of his third glass of wine. "Maybe you shouldn't be driving," she says.

He laughs. "I'm fine. Just tired. I'm sorry I don't remember having you in a workshop. Congratulations again on your book." He taps his bag. "I look forward to reading it," and he opens the door.

She knows she still has his copy of her book in her purse, and rather than remind him, or try to figure out something to write, she says thank you and that she hopes he'll enjoy it.

He opens his Chevy Tahoe and has to pull on the doorjamb to garner enough momentum to swing into the seat. He starts the vehicle and pulls down the visor, situates his glasses, and pulls the drive shaft to Drive. He waves as he pulls out, his steering slow and tentative. Eight years ago he was a symbol—a metaphor, in writing terms—of what she hoped for her future, but now she can see each of them for what they are: an old man and a younger woman. His career, while successful, has peaked.

Pam waves back and wonders when he'll remember that she has the book. Whether it'll be on the drive home—his temple starting to pulse from concentration as he drives in the dark—or if it will be later that night as he's crawling into bed, his wife's heavy hip nestled into the mattress. Perhaps it will be the next morning when he brushes his teeth. Or maybe never. Her book will remain a niggling in his conscious, one more thing he seems to be forgetting, like a black bloom started at the edge of his vision. Like those student names, the first euphoria of publication, his own infidelities—another thing receding into the past, just out of reach.

The Summer of Cancer

Every morning Tracy and I meet at nine thirty and put on our bikinis and coat our bodies with a super-secret concoction of baby oil and iodine. Then we spray Sun-In on the tops of our heads and then we flip our heads upside down and spray Sun-In at the roots. This way we get all of the hair and not just the top layer, which is what most people do and which is why their hair looks fake. We've nicknamed these months before our eighth-grade year "The Summer of Cancer."

Before this I didn't get what people thought was so great about laying out, why they devoted hours and hours and days and days to sweating on a blanket with nothing to do but sweat and squint, occasionally falling asleep and waking up to find they're covered in bugs, the grass pushed into their skin, even though they're not directly *on* the grass. Now spending hours on a towel in Tracy's backyard, I'm never bored. We talk about school and world news and Kirk Cameron and our hair, and her dad buys us any snacks we want. One day we had a contest to see how many Little Debbie Swiss Cake Rolls we could eat and Tracy won at nine. I could have kept going but chose to stop, and a half hour after announcing her victory, Tracy threw the Swiss Cake Rolls up in the toilet so it looked like cake soup. There is never an end to excitement in The Summer of Cancer.

Tracy's dad is very proud of how diligent we've become. Not only does he reward us with any snack we ask for, but if he's home during the day, which he is a lot, he'll bring them into the backyard on a TV tray along with Tabs and an extra bucket of ice for when the ice in our glasses melts. I'm not sure what it is that Tracy's dad—Mr. Mackelvoy, although he's asked me to call him Don— does, but it's something with computers, which he says are going to be really big in a few years. Tracy says when that happens she'll be able to wear Pepe jeans once and then throw them away like they're made of paper, but no one can tell what the future's going to bring. Right now it's The Summer of Cancer and Tracy and I are best friends that like to lie in the sun and eat snack cakes and laugh and laugh and laugh.

My mom and dad both work and they have no idea what it is that Tracy and I do all day. My mother would freak if she knew I was spending this much time in the sun, but it's there on my body at the end of each day, even though I've never tanned before. (As a kid I always burned then blistered then peeled then started over, but I realize now I just wasn't persistent enough to get to the tan underneath.) She doesn't question how many hours we are exposed to direct sunlight, how it is her daughter now has the skin of a Mexican when we're of Irish descent. That's what Tracy says: that I look like a Mexican, and even though I don't want people to think I really am, I know a compliment when I hear one. My dad doesn't say boo about my tan either, but this is normal. Ever since I got my period six months ago he acts like I don't have a body anymore, that I'm a daughter he can't touch or hug. I realized finally that he's afraid of my body in a way that makes me both proud and a little sad for him. Also, my parents spend most of their attention on my brother who is seven and has cerebral palsy really bad. He shakes when he talks and ends up with half of every meal on his bib. His name is James and even though he's seven, no one thinks to call him Jim or Jimmy.

The secret I've found to a good tan is variety. You need to vary the position in which you expose yourself to the sun, and you need to have more than one swimsuit so you can change it often so you don't develop tan lines. Sometimes, if we're pulling a double header lying out in the late morning through late afternoon, I'll wear three different suits during the day. Luckily, Tracy and I are the same size—meaning flat as boards—and I can borrow hers. I only have two suits but Tracy has nine. Even though it's a few years before computers get really big, Mr. Mackelvoy already buys her about anything she wants. He totally feels bad because her mother died in a lightning storm when Tracy was only eight, and even though Tracy knows it's wrong, she uses that guilt to her advantage to get swimsuits and Atari and really anything else she wants. In addition to varying the suits for an overall even tan, you need to flip not only from your front to your back, but to your sides too, with your exposed arm raised above your head. That's the key move that everyone forgets: lying on their side with their arm above their head.

By the beginning of August we're black as bears and the contrast of our hair, with all that Sun-In, makes us look even darker. Tracy and I are in her kitchen making peanut butter and Fluff sandwiches—they sound gross but they're really good if you like sweet—and Mr. Mackelvoy comes into the kitchen and asks if we want to go to the mall. School starts in three weeks. It's only half past eleven in the morning so we've barely gotten any time in on the towel, but we're not the type of girls to pass up a trip to the mall. It's dark in the kitchen because I've been staring in the sun since ten o'clock but I catch outlines of movement from Mr. Mackelvoy. He's a fidgety guy with hands like nervous birds, but he doesn't look old-old like my parents do. He slips his hands in his pockets and out again.

"We can't go until two," Tracy tells her dad. "We're laying out."

Mr. Mackelvoy nods, his fingers splayed on the counter, playing air-piano. "I thought you might want to get new swimsuits for this afternoon."

"Don't be stupid," Tracy says, her words muddied by the peanut butter. She talks like this to her dad all the time, saying rude things I wouldn't say to my own family. I don't say much to them at all. "We want to go at two." Other times Tracy will run to her father and throw herself at him—on his lap and into his arms until he's forced to drop the newspaper in his hand and pick her body up under the knees so she doesn't fall—and coo as if she's five years old. This is usually when she wants something, like pizza or the new tinted Clearasil or for him to leave or stay for the night.

"That's fine," Mr. Mackelvoy says and heads back to the basement where he keeps his computers and computer parts.

Outside, Tracy flips to her stomach with her arms raised and her feet flexed; people always forget about the bottoms of their feet. "I'm sorry my dad's such a toad," she says.

"It's fine," I say. "I don't mind." And I don't. It's nice that Mr. Mackelvoy wants to take us to the mall and the pool and out for ice cream, even though we make him sit in the car while we're at the Dairy Queen, ten feet away and acting like we've never seen him before in our lives. I used to order chocolate sundaes but Mr. Mackelvoy convinced me it was less calories to get a cone, and since I hate to jog or do aerobics, I'm happy eating my cone. He's the kind of dad who looks out for us and our figures, which is more than I can say for my own dad.

We lie in the sun until two thirty and then take quick showers, careful not to wash the Sun-In out of our hair, and then Mr. Mackelvoy takes us to the mall. Tracy lets him come in the mall but not inside the stores. He waits on a bench outside with all the really old men whose wives are picking up prescriptions at Walgreens or buying orthopedic shoes, while we spend hours and hours reading sex board games at Spencer Gifts and joke cards about farting and big boobs. We spend hours and hours and hours in there, and Mr. Mackelvoy just sits on the bench and waits for us.

Sometimes I get bored and anxious about his waiting but Tracy never does. She could keep her dad out there forever.

After Spencer Gifts we move on to Vanity where Tracy and I try on shirts with low-cut necklines that don't point to anything, but when we're done she waves a hand at her dad who is always watching us, and he comes in with his credit card and pays. On the way home she takes the purple top from the bag and slides it across the backseat toward me. "Really?" I say, and I'm super-excited because my parents buy my clothes at J. C. Penney. Tracy just shrugs and Mr. Mackelvoy shuttles us home in silence.

Tracy doesn't like to talk about her mom, and because Tracy is my best friend, I respect that. We have blank spots in our friendship, like staring at the sun, that include her mom and my brother and my parents and her dad. When Tracy's mom died Tracy was pulled out of school for a month, and I wonder now if that's when she first realized her father was a pushover, that just five more years in the future she'd get him to buy her all the swimsuits she wants. My mother told me at the time that I had to remember the whole picture—Tracy might get out of school for a month but she no longer had a mother—but that's hard to do when you're eight. Now it's easier for me to see that Tracy really does have it best. She's over her mother dying, while I've got a mother who doesn't talk to me and doesn't even care that I'm giving myself cancer every day lying in the sun. Tracy has Mr. Mackelvoy—Don—who buys her swimsuits and Little Debbies and treats her like she's the best girl in the world when even I can tell she's a complete brat. If I were his daughter I wouldn't make him spend hours outside of Spencer Gifts even though he doesn't seem to mind.

Two weeks before school starts, Tracy and I are sweating in the hot Colorado sun, which seems to be getting hotter and hotter thanks to global warming, which people are just starting to blab about. I'm glad that Sun-In works as a pump not an aerosol so it's not destroying the ozone. Tracy turns on her stomach and looks at me and I glance at the stopwatch; we've got eight minutes until the next flip. "My dad needs a girlfriend," she says.

"Ew." In all the years I've known Mr. Mackelvoy I've never known him to have a girlfriend and I can't imagine why Tracy would want her dad to date someone when it would mean less attention for her. A girlfriend would definitely cut into her swimsuit budget.

And then Tracy says something that really surprises me: "I wish I had your dad."

My dad doesn't speak to me, much less to Tracy. When she stays at my house and we're up at eleven thirty on Friday night watching *Friday Night Videos*, he'll sometimes come into the kitchen, which is right off the living room, and make himself a snack. He never, ever makes one for us. When he sees us there he is always surprised. Not just to see Tracy—like we didn't just all have dinner together a few hours before—but me too, as if he's surprised to have a daughter at all. My dad looks tired and thin in his worn pajamas with his hair messed up and his bloodshot eyes. He'll point at us with the chicken leg in his hand or the ham sandwich and then go upstairs to check on James, who sleeps in a crib we had specially made. "Why would you want my dad?" I ask. "He's a complete toad."

Tracy shrugs and in complete violation of the rules sits up and slacks her shoulders across her knees, which will result in a wicked crisscross pattern on her legs if she stays like that. "But at least he's like a dad," she says. "Dads are supposed to ignore their daughters." She squints at me, like she's looking at the sun, and I feel myself begin to perspire even more. "My dad's so lonely it's made him sick, Em."

"Like cancer?"

She crinkles her nose and lies back down and flings a sweaty arm across her eyes with a *slap* noise. "Kind of," she says. "Like cancer." She lifts her arm and half-opens one eye. "Never mind okay, Em? Forget I said anything about it."

At home that night, my mother makes a meal from a box and serves it with canned green beans. James doesn't like canned green beans and keeps his mouth shut against the spoon, shaking his thin head from side to side. My father watches the TV in the corner, all the while scoping the beans into the spoon again and again until finally James opens his mouth. I want to grab my dad's wrist and make him look at James's face and see that he doesn't want to eat them, but I don't want to eat them either—what kid does?—so I keep to myself, eat the rest of my beans, and when dinner's done I go to my room to look at Tracy's leftover magazines that she's already read.

A few mornings later Tracy calls and tells me her dad's not feeling well and she's going to stay home and take care of him, so I sneak to the library and look up cancer. It's a word surrounded by many other words that I don't understand or want to think about: malignant, carcinogens, radiation, oncogene, tumor. Even though we joke about The Summer of Cancer it now doesn't seem so funny, and rather than punishing us, God has decided to take it out on Mr. Mackelvoy which doesn't seem fair to me but is the way God works. Just ask James, who supposedly has a super-high IQ, but who really cares when his limbs are growing like deformed branches and his cheeks are so lax it's hard to look him in the face?

Later when I confess about the library to Tracy, she laughs and tells me that we don't get to decide who gets cancer or not or who gets struck by lightning. She holds a thin brown arm in the air. "Besides. No one as good looking as us ever dies of some fuddy old cancer."

The week before school starts I'm over at the Mackelvoys laying out, when Tracy asks me to go inside and find a different tape. We've been listening to *Seven and the Ragged Tiger* for an hour now, and while we agree there's nothing dreamier than Simon LeBon, we can't take another round of "The Reflex." "Sure," I say. Tracy is used to being waited on by her father, and since she's so nice to me—loaning me her swimsuits like the pink-and-green-striped halter bikini I'm wearing right now and getting her father to buy Oatmeal Crème Pies, which she thinks are gross—I don't mind doing favors for her.

Even though it's August and we've been laying out for months, my eyes have gotten no better at adjusting to the darkness when I come inside from the backyard. I squint into the kitchen and see a blob where the table is, blobby appliances by the walls. I stick a hand out and feel for the breakfast bar that I know is just inside the doorway but it's soft and fabric and I hear a sharp intake of breath and pull my hand away as soon as I realize I've touched Mr. Mackelvoy and not the marble counter top.

"Sorry," I say. "I can't see from the sun."

"It's fine, Emily," Mr. Mackelvoy says quietly, and he looks at me for a moment from blonde head to painted toe, admiring my tan. "That's Tracy's suit, isn't it?" he says.

I look down at the pink-and-green bikini, suddenly self-conscious of how small it is, how weird it is to have a conversation in a bikini when the person you're talking to is wearing pants and a shirt and even loafers. "She said I could borrow it," I say and pull down the top at my side where it continually rides up because even though my chest is small, it's still a little bigger than Tracy's.

"Of course, that's fine. I just wondered if you had the same suit." I glance outside and Tracy's still on her towel, her knees wobbling a bit to create a breeze because it's August and hotter than stink outside. "Are you excited to start school next week?" he asks.

"As if."

Mr. Mackelvoy laughs at my response like I am truly witty, then moves to the fridge and pulls out two Tabs, handing one to me. "It's been nice having you around these past few months," he says. "We've been lonely since Tracy's mother died. That was a hard time on the both of us."

"I'm sorry." I fidget with the Tab in my hands. I don't know what to do with an adult who will talk to me as if he too has problems. My parents—their biggest problem squirming in a crib one room away—don't talk to me at all. "You must miss her a ton."

"I do," he continues. "I don't know what I'd do without Tracy." He pulls back the tab on the soda and the fizzing sound echoes in the room. "I love her a lot."

And suddenly it doesn't seem so right that he loves her so much, even if she gets Atari and swimsuits—but when I look at what I'm getting, which is nothing, I don't know how to compare. Maybe he loves her because he doesn't have anyone else, but then why, if my parents have each other and James and me, do they still seem to have so little?

"Emily?" he whispers. "May I give you a hug?"

Mr. Mackelvoy looks at me with such empty need. Were my parents to ask I would give them anything, anything at all, and so when Mr. Mackelvoy—Don—asks for something as simple as a hug, no matter how odd when I'm in Tracy's swimsuit and he's in pants and loafers, I can do nothing but say yes.

He sets down his soda and moves slowly across the length of the kitchen, his body like a shape shifter in the blinding whiteness of the sun that is streaming through the glass-paned door. "Your friendship means a lot to Tracy," he says and he puts his hands on my shoulders. His hands are cold from the soda and refreshing against my hot skin, still baking and slick from the baby oil. His hands slide across my naked back as he pulls me in for a hug. "You're a good friend to me too," he says, his breath muffled in my hair, but also surprisingly cool.

"Thanks," I say and bring my palms to his shoulders, afraid to touch him but then melting in, so glad to be leaning against someone solid, or someone at all, not only a dad, but a person who cares.

There's a clamor from outside as Tracy pulls back the glass patio door, the pane vibrating in its tracks as it bounces against the wall. She runs toward us, her slick feet smacking on the linoleum.

"What are you doing?" she shouts and I break away, surprised to see she's staring at her father and not me. I wonder how she can see us at all after staring at the sun outside, and I think maybe she hasn't focused yet, that she thinks she's staring at me but it's him.

"Tracy," Mr. Mackelvoy begins, but it's too late. Tracy has run across the kitchen, her feet slapping on the floor and then muffled as she pounds her way up the carpeted stairs. "I'm sorry," Mr. Mackelvoy continues. "It might be best if you went home."

I place my unopened Tab on the breakfast bar before I walk to the patio door. "Should I change first?" I ask. "Leave Tracy her suit?"

Mr. Mackelvoy shakes his head no. "You can keep it, Emily. I'll buy her another."

When school starts a week later, it's obvious to me that Tracy and I are no longer best friends. I called her every day for four days straight but she wouldn't speak with me, and after a while even Mr. Mackelvoy wouldn't answer, and I was left leaving messages on the machine like I'm begging to have her back, and then *that* gets too humiliating so I just hang up.

But I stay diligent about my tan, out in the yard for four to six hours a day, upping it to eight the weekend before school starts when my parents have to take James to Children's Hospital in Denver. My grandmother comes to stay with me but has no idea what's going on, so she just knits inside while I work on my cancer, which won't put me in a crib or twist my limbs but is just as serious as cerebral palsy.

On Monday when I get to school, everyone tells me I look fantastic, not only with my tan skin but how blonde my hair is. One girl, Sarah Massey, tells me I look older than some sophomores. Tracy doesn't so much as glance at me as she walks past, and I can't really blame her. She must have spent the last week locked inside, completely abandoning The Summer of Cancer, because her color's already started to fade and her true paleness is fighting its way back.

By lunch everyone seems to have forgotten how dark I am, and they've moved on to other important matters—like whose breasts have grown the most over summer—but I know if I can get on the towel from three thirty to five after school and still put in my long days on the weekends that I'll be able to sustain this color, and even come winter it won't be entirely lost. Before long Tracy and everyone else will be dying to know how I've done it—how I've stayed so tan—and my parents will start to ask some serious questions. Because if I've understood one thing from The Summer of Cancer it's that you have to lay there day after day, hour after hour, baking, sweating, and waiting, and if you are diligent enough and want it bad enough, you can end up with skin so far from where you started that it will only be a matter of time before someone becomes concerned and insists you come out of the sun or compliments you on your dedication.

Feather the Nest

Meredith was raking her yard when she came across the bird—a tiny thing with a heart like an anxious eye tick. She leaned over and plucked the bird from the ground. It sat in her palm, no feathers, the skin stretched tight across the ribcage, but everywhere else, such as around the neck and joints, the skin was gathered and puckered like an old man's knuckle.

She looked up but didn't see a nest in the oak tree. As a child she'd found a mother cat eating her young, swallowing the tiny bodies whole as if to get them back to the womb. Meredith had snatched the last two kittens away from the nest of straw and T-shirts she'd set up in her parents' garage and moved the kittens inside and fed them with an eyedropper. The first died within a week, the other lived for almost a year until her parents took him in to be neutered, and the cat died from anesthesia and a hole in his heart. The vet told her it was most likely a deficiency in the entire litter; the mother had been performing an act of mercy. Meredith didn't know what to do with the bird, still alive in her hand. She couldn't imagine it would live much longer and hoped she hadn't ruined its chances by scooping it up. Was it birds that recognized the scent of a human on their babies and wouldn't come back? Was that an old wives' tale?

She tore open a bag of mulch Mark had bought to put under the rocks and reached in for a handful of the soft twigs and dirt, the smell of earth thick in her throat. While she waited for him to return from Lowe's with more red rocks to surround the sweetspire bushes, she made a nest on the ground and laid the bird on its side. The doorbell rang and Grover started barking at the edge of the fence. Meredith glanced at her watch. It was just before 9:00 a.m.—too early for the mail. She wove her way through the house—the darkness contorted by bright spots after the sunshine outside—and answered the door.

"Why did you ring the doorbell?" she said to Mark, and he pushed her to the side on his way to the living room.

"Forgot my keys in the truck." He turned on the TV, punching in a news station. "There's been an accident in New York. A plane. It flew into the World Trade Center."

"Was a woman driving?" Meredith joked, knowing Mark always cursed women drivers on the road. On the screen, a woman with perfect makeup recited from a teleprompter, her voice modulated with newscaster overemphasis. Meredith and Mark listened as the woman told them about the accident—a commercial airliner, American flight 11, had flown into the North Tower—and then the newscaster dropped her veneer, and a hand flew up to her mouth as her other hand pushed at her ear. There was a second plane.

Meredith's first thought: *Where are my babies?* "Oh, Jesus," she said. "Oh God."

"It can't be an accident," Mark said.

Grant was at work eight miles away, his children Sophie and Clark in school. Elias, her momma's boy, had been at the bakery since four o'clock that morning—Meredith had talked to him an hour ago about whether he and Joanie would like some old furniture they were clearing out. Sarah. Where was Sarah? She rarely flew for work—only academic conferences once or twice a semester, and Meredith knew she had one coming up but it was in Florida. Could Sarah be in New York? Was there any reason? Sometimes flight patterns made no sense. One time Meredith flew from Kansas City to Phoenix and ended up in Atlanta. She thought Sarah's conference was later in the month, but maybe she was wrong.

She picked up the phone, surprised there was a ring tone, the world still functioning at its most basic level. She called Sarah at home and her daughter answered, her voice incredulous. "Can you believe it?" Sarah said, and Meredith nearly wept with relief.

"Thank god," Meredith said to Mark after she'd hung up with their daughter, knowing she would call Elias and Grant after all, that she needed to hear their voices. "Thank god everyone's okay."

Mark looked at her queerly. "How can you say that?" he said. "Jesus, Meredith. Hundreds of people are dead."

She wanted all of her children home as soon as they could come. Grant, back in Kansas City since his divorce, was already over all the time, and Elias, just an hour away, visited every other week or so with fresh bread in hand. Sarah would be the toughest to convince, Meredith figured. Sarah was only a few weeks into a new semester, Christmas and another visit only three months away. Meredith was surprised when Sarah said she'd be happy to come, was the end of the month okay? The last weekend? And would it be all right if she brought a friend? Meredith said all of that would be wonderful and to send her flight information so she and Mark could pick them up. "We're going to drive, actually," Sarah said.

"Nine hours?" But Meredith was too relieved to question it, too glad to have her daughter on the ground.

Of course it would be great to see her boys and grandkids, but Sarah was the one Meredith saw so rarely. She had moved away, created a life for herself, had cut the diaphanous apron strings Meredith wanted to imagine still stretching from her to her children. She had not had to mother Sarah as she had the boys, who were like bright, open, empty boxes to her. As a child, Sarah was willful; as a teenager, unknowable. Meredith used to lie awake wondering what her daughter thought about, who she spent her time with at school. She had always known all of her sons' friends. She and Mark ran the house everyone referred to as "The Hub."

One afternoon when Sarah was in high school, Meredith left her part-time job with a headache and came home to find a boy she'd never heard of—Jasper Day—sitting on their living room couch watching *Jeopardy* while Sarah made them turkey sandwiches in the kitchen. It had been like watching a future Sarah, a stranger, play house. Jasper had been surprisingly good at the game show, getting more questions right than Meredith, although she reasoned this made sense, that many of the questions revolved around the arcane information you learned in school and then promptly forgot. Sarah, already a history buff, stayed silent even when the category was American Presidents. After Jasper left, Sarah was more talkative than usual, telling Meredith about a ruckus in the lunchroom that day, and Meredith had reveled in the inconsequential minutia she was rarely privy to. Sarah was in her thirties now, and Meredith had heard nothing of Faris, the person coming home with her from Colorado, where Sarah was an assistant professor at Deridan College. "Faris," she'd said to Mark. "What an interesting name."

Planning for the visit, Meredith washed all the sheets and windows, cut fall flowers from the garden. The night of September 11th, she had gone outside and found the bird still in the nest she'd made. They had abandoned the yard work that day, the gray bags of mulch like tombstones in the yard, a wheelbarrow of red rocks next to them. Of course the bird was dead. It couldn't have been more than a day old, maybe a few hours, and had fallen to the earth, unaided, with a thud. They finished their landscaping over the next two weeks, and each time she went to the garden it reminded Meredith of the tragedy, the towers falling in a loop through every American's mind.

Sarah and Faris arrived on a Saturday in time for dinner, the rest of the family already gathered, the grandkids running helter-skelter through the house.

Faris was driving, and as Sarah climbed out of the car she said the road trip was like an old-fashioned honeymoon. "Just like you two had," she said and kissed her dad on the cheek. Two days after they had gotten married, Meredith and Mark left for San Francisco from Topeka so Mark could start an entry-level job at an architectural firm. They'd driven from Kansas in three days and Meredith remembered feeling like such a stranger as a wife, she'd been too embarrassed to tell Mark she needed to stop and go to the bathroom. She was careful not to drink too much water or coffee on the road, and their first night in the hotel she drank three glasses of water before bed, then spent half the night up peeing. The next day she fell asleep in the car and awoke to find drool on her chin, Mark grinning in the driver's seat, telling her she snored.

"It's nice to meet you," Meredith said and shook hands with Faris while Mark enveloped him in a hug. His skin was a rich brown, his hair a wing of black. Meredith put her arms around her daughter as the front door opened, Sophie and Clark hot on the trail for gifts. They loved their Aunt Sarah, and as little as Sarah called home, Grant told his mom that Sarah was sure to call a few times a week when he had the kids, to wish them pleasant dreams and hear about their days. Since the terrorist attacks, Sophie had woken up almost every night with a nightmare. At six she didn't understand what had happened, but she understood the anxiety that ran through her house and through her school, through the shoulders of every adult she knew. The last time she would have felt such a thing, her father had moved out. By now they all knew about Bin Laden and Al-Qaeda, a man and organization none of them had heard of three weeks before. They'd all watched George Bush give his speech through a megaphone at Ground Zero and wondered how many more planes had been scheduled. Meredith had an uneasy feeling it wasn't over, that they all had to stay on high alert.

Mark hugged Sarah again. "I'll get your bags from the car."

"That's why I brought Faris, to bring in the suitcases." Faris laughed and made a right angle at the elbow, holding his arm in the air so they could all see how spindly it was. Was he Muslim, Meredith wondered, but how to ask without asking?

Faris said, "I'm not saying she chose well, but I can at least bring in some bags."

The men came back in and put the suitcases in the foyer. Grant and Elias got up from the sofa where they had been watching a football game and bear-hugged their sister, shook hands with Faris. Meredith had been worrying for a week what to do with the bags, if she should put them in the same room or separate rooms. Her daughter was over thirty, for god's sake, but as old-fashioned as it was, she couldn't imagine letting Sarah sleep with a man in her house without being married. She remembered Jasper Day on the couch, the surprise of seeing him there when she came through the door. "Hey," he'd said. "You must be Sarah's mom." Had Sarah brought someone home during college, when she was twenty, the answer would have been easy: separate rooms, no question. But now? She left the bags in the foyer.

Settling in the living room with the game now on mute, they found out Faris and Sarah had met at Deridan a year earlier at new-faculty orientation. He was a lecturer in economics (Sarah was in history), finishing up his dissertation from the University of Colorado. Meredith worked to keep her face neutral yet engaged; a year before and this was the first she was hearing of it? She was dizzy with the idea of her daughter's life one state over, a life she apparently knew nothing about. When Mark asked if anyone would like a drink, Faris put a hand to Sarah's back.

"We have some news," Sarah said. "I was thinking we'd wait and announce it tomorrow after you'd had a chance to get to know each other a bit more, but here you go: I'm pregnant." She smiled at them each individually, starting with Faris and moving to Mark and Meredith, who was halfway to the kitchen to get the wine. "You're going to be grandparents again."

Mark reacted quickly, gathering Sarah in a hug and spinning her through the room, then making a production of setting her down and putting his hands to her belly to make sure the baby was okay. He rested both hands against Sarah's cotton shirt as if he were giving a blessing.

Sarah looked over at Meredith. "Mom? Are you okay?" Meredith put a hand to her face and felt that she was sweating.

"Of course. I'm fine. This is wonderful news." She hoped she managed to inject enough feeling into her voice to pull this off.

Sarah laughed. "Are you upset?"

Meredith regained herself. "Of course not. More reasons to come visit you. I couldn't be happier." She stood up to hug Sarah and then Faris. *Who is this man?* "When are you due?" Sarah told them in April—almost three months along!—and Meredith asked what she'd do about spring semester.

"There's more," Sarah said. "We've decided we don't want our baby raised by strangers, so at the end of this semester, I'm resigning."

Meredith looked up, startled. "What?"

"I never thought this would be the job I stayed at," Sarah continued, "and if I were to get tenure it would mean I was basically stuck. And since Faris likes teaching so much more than I do, he can do that while I stay home and care for the baby. And work on turning my diss into a book."

"What about things like insurance?"

"One more *tiny* thing," Sarah said, and held her thumb and forefinger a half inch apart. Faris leaned forward, a hand on Sarah's knee.

"It's a little late to make an honest woman of her, but I'm doing what I can," and Meredith saw white spots in her vision.

"You're getting married?" she said. "But, we're just meeting you!"

"I think Grandma needs to sit down," Mark said and put an arm on Meredith's elbow to lead her to a chair. She pulled it away more abruptly than planned and laughed to compensate.

"I'm fine. Really. It's all such a surprise. Here we are just meeting Faris and now he's family."

"It's my fault," Sarah said. "We talked about Faris coming with me for Christmas last year but decided you might not like someone intruding on all the traditions."

"Yes," Meredith said. "This is much less intrusive."

"I think it's great," Mark said. "Just great. Something like the World Trade Center can happen in this world, but you can also have a baby. We're happy for you. We really are." Meredith felt a gentle pressure on her shoulder.

"It's just such a surprise," Meredith repeated. "A baby, you quitting your job. A wedding." She turned to Sarah. "Are you even having a wedding?"

"Not really," Sarah admitted. "We figured we'd just get married by the justice of the peace. Maybe stay overnight at a nice hotel in Denver." She laughed and put a hand on her stomach. "Not like he can do any more damage."

"Are we invited?" Meredith asked and Sarah shrugged.

"It's only going to be like a five-minute deal, but if you want to come, you can. That or we can have a friend tape it."

"I can buy a new dress to sit on the sofa and watch it," Meredith said. "The mother of the bride."

"Bottom line," Mark said, in a voice that let Meredith know they were wrapping up the conversation. "We're happy for you, we are." Meredith sat down, the seat behind her rising to meet her. Somehow, without her knowing it, Mark had steered her to a chair after all.

Meredith woke up that night in a sweat, her T-shirt clinging to her chest. Ever since menopause ten years earlier, she'd awoken occasionally with hot flashes if she was under stress or had had too much to drink. The night of the attacks, she'd climbed out of bed drenched, her shoulders and back like fire. All through her forties she'd dreaded menopause, knowing it meant she was getting old, and while she was reasonably past her child-bearing years, she'd felt she would still be young, still be a woman, until it hit. After menopause she realized she didn't feel like less of a woman, just a crankier one, a hotter one. The injustice was that while her periods had stopped, the hot flashes had continued, one inconvenience of womanhood exchanged for another.

She pulled the T-shirt away and swung her feet over the bed. Downstairs, she got a glass of ice water and settled on the couch, resting the cold glass against her feet. Mark had left the TV on, a habit he'd had for two decades that coincided, she had realized, with Sarah going away to college. He couldn't stand the hum and creak of an empty house, empty except for them. Sarah and Faris were upstairs but the boys had gone home for the night. If it had been up to only him, Mark would have had four babies, or five, maybe not stopping until a baker's dozen.

She picked up the remote and changed channels until she found the soothing voice of Tom Brokaw, another midwesterner, telling her about the country's wreckage. As many as six hundred people had been killed instantly when the towers went down—including the suicide bombers—but the body count was still rising; it would be months, even years, before they had a final tally of almost three thousand. In the glow of the TV, Meredith flipped channels, finally settling on a panel of experts discussing Bush's response to the disaster. When John Kennedy was shot, she and Mark had been married for two years and Grant was a few months old. For Christmas that year, Mark had bought her a new range oven, something woefully out of their budget, and when RFK was assassinated five years later, they'd taken a family vacation for more than they could afford to the Grand Canyon. She wondered if Sarah's life decisions weren't a similar reaction to 9/11—a reshuffling of priorities and happiness, a determination to live in the moment. Nine-eleven: that's what the newscasters were calling it, what they'd call it for the rest of their lives. Maybe Sarah keeping the baby, the marriage, quitting her career, it was all just a reaction against this national tragedy, a world without sense. She wondered how she could ask without seeming hopeful.

And Faris. Over dinner, he had told them he was a first-generation Indian American, that his parents had moved to Boston from outside Bihar Sharif a few years before he was born. Meredith wondered if he had learned this casual way of reassuring others of his past—*I am one of you*—in the last few weeks or, more likely, if he'd practiced it his entire life. Either way, she'd been relieved. She never wanted to consider herself wary of outsiders—who did?—but this was her daughter she was worried about, her own child. Meredith wanted nothing for Sarah but Sarah's own happiness, but how was it Meredith could have so little idea what that meant?

She heard a creak on the stairs and turned to see Faris come through the foyer. He wore a blank expression, his face slack from sleep. He spotted her on the sofa and jumped. "You startled me. I didn't expect anyone to be up."

"Me either," Meredith said. "Can I get you anything?"

"No, no. I didn't get up in the middle of the night expecting to be waited on," he said.

I should hope not. "I didn't wake you, did I?"

"I'm a light sleeper. Most nights I'm up three, four times. It's taken Sarah some getting used to." Meredith had decided, in the end, to put their bags in the same room. It seemed ridiculous at this point to do anything else.

From the living room, Meredith heard Faris open a few kitchen cupboards, the clink as he pulled down a glass, the hum and drop of ice from the ice machine, and finally the tinkle of water. He came back in and pointed at the glass by Meredith's feet. "You want some more?"

"I'm fine. I just like the coolness."

He sat next to her on the sofa and pointed his glass at the television. "It's still so hard to believe."

"Isn't it?" She didn't want to make small talk about 9/11 or about anything. "I'm surprised to hear Sarah's quitting her job."

He brought the water to his mouth and gulped down half the glass, and Meredith wondered if she and Mark had turned into old people who kept the house five degrees too warm. "Me too. I told her we could hire a nanny, or if she really wanted one of us home, I'd be the one."

"So you agree it's a mistake?"

"I agree it's a surprise."

Meredith loved her children more than anything in the world—more than Mark, more than herself—but they were such a responsibility, so relentless. Sarah had no idea what she was getting into. Every moment she was a mother as surely as she was breathing. The reason she had opened her house to every child in the neighborhood, the reason they'd been The Hub, was so she could keep track of her children, literally lay her hands on them at any given moment. That hadn't worked with Sarah, who, as a teenager, began to live her life away from home, already moving toward a future Meredith could only guess. Meredith moved the glass from her feet to her face. The hot flash was over, her face now covered in cool sweat.

"The pregnancy wasn't planned," he said. "But we're happy about it. A happy accident." They watched TV for a few minutes in silence until Faris stood up and said he was going to try and get back to sleep.

"I'll see you in the morning," she said.

"We've loaded a lot on your plate," he said. "This on top of what's happened," and he motioned to the TV. It took Meredith a moment to realize he meant 9/11 not the car commercial for Chevy that was on at the moment. She remembered how, when she heard, she had been concerned only for her family, the hundreds dead on the periphery of her mind.

"Well good night, then," he said, and Meredith held out her hand to take his glass.

In the morning, despite a headache from lack of sleep, Meredith got up early and headed outside. She and Mark had finished the landscaping before the kids came home, but she still needed to aerate the lawn before the first frost. She slipped on the aerating shoes that Mark had bought her for their thirty-something anniversary from a *SkyMall* magazine and began walking the length of the yard. She wondered if a national tragedy had hit that May, if she would have been able to get a new washing machine.

The back screen door opened and Mark stuck his head out, dressed in running shorts and a sweatshirt. "I'm going," he said. He ran four miles nearly every day since they'd married forty-two years before. She couldn't think of any routine she'd kept up that long, other than cooking his meals, cleaning his house, worrying about their children. "Faris is coming with me."

"What about Sarah?"

"In the kitchen."

"I'll come in," Meredith said, and slipped off the aerating shoes. Inside, she put a pan of cinnamon rolls in the oven that Elias had dropped off that morning—Sarah's favorite—and flipped on the kitchen counter TV, a habit she'd developed in the last few weeks. She and Sarah stood in front of the small TV in the same position: their left arms tucked under the elbows of their right, holding their cups to their mouths—coffee for Meredith, milk for Sarah. "I still can't believe it," Meredith said, staring at the screen. Some regular broadcasting had resumed, but the morning talk-show hosts were still finding their feet, balancing the respectful tone of national tragedy with information on potty training a cat or how to bake muffins that turned out every time (fresh baking soda was the key).

"I can't watch anymore," Sarah said and turned it off. "It's been 9/11 for three weeks straight. Even something this watered-down makes me too sad."

"You used to love the news," Meredith mused. "Even as a little kid. I'd turn that on and you'd watch it just as happily as *Sesame Street*." She put a hand on Sarah's arm. "Are you sure about giving up your career? A baby is one thing, but quitting your job?"

Sarah took another drink of milk, grimacing. "I don't like it," she said. "The job. I'm interested in colonial history, obviously, and I love researching it, but I don't want to teach. I hate my students. One of them came up to me a week after a paper was due and asked when he could hand it in. I told him the deadline had passed and he said, so do we make a new deadline? I said, 'No, that ship has sailed.' You know what he said?"

"What?"

"'That's odd.'"

"But that's just one student."

"Our chairs and deans tell us part of our job is to feather the nest, help these kids through the transition from home. What's that got to do with being a college professor? And the committee work. It's just so many papers getting pushed around."

"You act like you're surprised by all this. What did you think the job was going to look like? Isn't this what you were in school for all those years?"

Sarah shrugged. "I don't know. I thought it would be me and my colleagues sitting around pontificating about history, about what a cad William Berkeley was, but I'm the only one who gives a shit about that. The department's so small that I'm the only one who's ever heard of him because we're so busy trying to cover the Magna Carta."

Meredith felt a surge of hope. "It sounds like what you want is a bigger university. One with more lively colleagues, a better batch of students."

Sarah shook her head. "What I want is to stay home and raise babies." She smiled at her mom. "I want what you had."

Meredith felt a tightening in her chest and shook her head. "You don't want that, trust me."

Sarah swatted Meredith on the arm. "Mom!"

"Do you remember that year I dropped you and your brothers off at Catholic Bible school? The summer you got pinkeye? The year Elias broke his arm and Grant broke his leg? I'd never been in that church in my life; we're Lutheran for god's sake. I was driving by one day, and the three of you were screaming in the back and I'd just had it. I pulled into the parking lot, marched in with you three, and signed you up."

Sarah laughed. "I loved that Bible school."

"By the end of August I was ready to kill myself, and that was when you were in school. Never mind when I had three of you at home under the age of six." Meredith marveled now that she'd done it—raised three citizens of the world.

"If you were in one of my classes I'd tell you to think about your audience. Am I really the one to tell this to, how much you hated being a mother?"

Is that what I've been telling her? She remembered that week of Bible camp, how relieved she was to be responsible for no one but herself. Two of her children had already been mangled on her watch that summer—Elias on the monkey bars, Grant on a bike. That week she'd dropped the kids off each morning, gone back home, and walked through the silent halls of her house. By Wednesday she'd figured out to take off her clothes and put on her pajamas, folding the skirt and blouse over a chair so they wouldn't wrinkle when she lay down to watch TV. Right there, in the middle of the day.

Even so, all week, she would keep an ear out for the phone in case the church called with bad news. She would lay in the quiet and wonder who these people were, the ones now watching her children. Each time someone in the neighborhood passed by outside, their dog Rocco would explode in a sudden and territorial barking fit, and Meredith's heart would clamor in her chest.

Nine-eleven had reminded her of those early years of raising her children—the constant vigilance, the worry. The feeling that everything at any moment could be taken away. She didn't hate being a mother; she loved it too much. It nearly killed her.

"I have a confession to make too," Sarah said. "You remember my best friend, Mary Beth Oxindine?" She went to that church; Sarah had manipulated the week of camp. How she had arranged this, Meredith didn't know—in her memory she'd driven by the church on a fluke, down Parcel Street, didn't she drive that every day?—but she didn't doubt it for a second.

"How in the world?" Meredith asked.

"That was the summer I wanted to be a nun," Sarah said fondly and Meredith nodded, knowing her daughter would never tell her how she arranged it.

"You wore your shirt over your head for weeks like a habit. Told me everything I did was a sin." Even then she had no control over her child and what her future would be. At best she tried to steer her children in the right direction. "I think you need to rethink quitting your job," she said. "Make a list of pros and cons."

Sarah pointed out the window to where Mark and Faris were turning onto their block, Mark's breathing even and Faris's labored as he trailed behind the much older man. She stood up with one hand on her belly and the other in the air to wave at Faris and her father. "Don't you get it, Mom? I've already quit. I'm done at the end of the semester."

They stayed one more night, Faris rising the next morning to go running with Mark despite the smell of Ben-Gay wafting from his skin. Meredith laid in bed listening to the sounds in her own kitchen, Sarah making an egg-white omelet on Meredith's stove. She'd woken in the night again and watched more coverage on 9/11. Everyone was still looking for the new angle, and in this show they were discussing the backgrounds of the suicide bombers, what leads someone to kill others and themselves for a cause, as if they could pinpoint it so easily. Meredith knew, eventually, they'd find a way to blame the mothers.

When she came downstairs, Sarah was leaning against the sink, drinking a glass of milk. "I'm sorry we have to go back so soon," she said. "I wish you had more time to get to know Faris. And I'm sorry about the surprise of it all. We didn't mean to be laying so much on you at once."

Meredith closed her robe and waved a hand to dismiss what her daughter said. She had purposefully not sulked the day before, after Sarah gave her the news of already quitting her job. They'd played Monopoly and Pitch in the afternoon; she'd made Sarah's favorite meal of lasagna for dinner, the same as she had planned. Sarah knew Meredith well enough though to know her mother was still upset, and Meredith knew Sarah at least well enough to pretend it didn't matter. "Never mind," she said. "I'm happy for you."

Sarah put her arm around her mother. "It's okay if you're not."

Meredith smiled and poured her coffee, the bitter taste hot and welcome. "You two don't teach today, I take it?" It was Monday.

"Faris doesn't, but I do. I e-mailed my students and told them to keep reading. I'll be back on Wednesday."

Meredith set down her coffee. "For god's sake, Sarah, at least try to finish the semester with some decorum in case you need a reference."

"They just give you the baby whether you're qualified or not," she said. "I don't need to worry about a reference."

"You never know what you'll want—"

Sarah cut her off. "Do you remember why I decided not to be a nun?"

Meredith looked at her, confused. "We weren't even Catholic."

"That wasn't it. I could have converted. It's because I couldn't have a baby. I found out you couldn't get married and have a baby and I decided to give it up." She rubbed her belly, something she had done dozens of times during the visit although she probably didn't realize it. Meredith knew Sarah was right; even as a child she would have gone through the years of catechism learning the rules of the church if that's what she wanted. Sarah's determination hadn't changed. "I'm in my midthirties, over-educated. I live in a town where the best place to meet men is a bar, but somehow I managed to find Faris and get pregnant and now I get to have a baby."

What Meredith would have given to be in that situation—no kids in her thirties, no husband to care for, no shoes to pick up in the living room but her own. How easy life would have been, how untethered. Who would she be without her children? Faris might believe the baby had been unplanned, but Meredith knew her daughter well enough to know that wasn't the case. She reveled in this: knowing her daughter better than Faris.

Faris came downstairs, his black hair slick from a shower. "We should get going," he said. "We've got a long drive ahead."

"We didn't want to fly after 9/11," Sarah explained. "Two days after it happened, Faris's sister was strip-searched in DC. They detained her for almost eight hours, her and the other brown people."

"It's still such a shock," Mark said and Meredith agreed. Men raised by mothers had flown planes into buildings. She imagined these women halfway around the world, their foreign eyes peering out from their burkas. On the show she'd watched the night before, the reporters had speculated they were proud of their children for dying for what they believed in, but what mother, no matter the cause, could accept her child's death? At the thought, Meredith felt grief scrabble its way up her throat.

She shook her head—her child was alive, a grandchild on the way—but the grief was still there, a connection to these mothers. With a start she realized this was now a connection to Sarah too. "Call me when you get there," she said. "Let us know you made it in one piece."

"I know, I know," Sarah said, and she turned to Faris. "She's been saying it since I turned sixteen."

"Just call and tell your mother you're home," Meredith said.

She and Mark followed Faris and Sarah to the car, and Mark lifted the suitcase into the trunk. It was another small thing they had taught their daughter and that she followed to this day: store your suitcase in the trunk when you travel so people won't assume you're carrying large sums of money. Maybe it was ridiculous. People would assume what they'd assume. Already their neighbor had decorations up for Halloween, the scarecrow in the yard plastic and ridiculous, although at least one night each October Meredith forgot it was there and was frightened half to death when she was out walking Grover, a stranger loose in the neighborhood.

"I love you," she said to Sarah, but it was Faris she took in her arms and told to watch out for her daughter, to make sure she got enough sleep.

"I can't tell her what to do any more than you can," he joked and Meredith supposed that was true. He climbed in the driver's seat, Sarah in the passenger's, and turned on the car. "It was nice meeting you," he said, and Sarah laughed at the banality of this statement after what they'd unloaded.

They share the same sense of humor, Meredith thought. That's good. Mark opened his arm and she instinctively leaned into his thin chest, a comfortable hollow for the last forty years. Faris backed up and she remembered taking off on that honeymoon all those years ago, her parents in the driveway. "Call us when you get there," her mother had surely yelled, but for the life of her, Meredith couldn't remember if she had obliged.

The Winning Ticket

In the summer of 1984, three weeks before the Olympics were to begin, the Russians pulled out of the games. I was eleven at the time, recently transplanted with my family from Lincoln, Nebraska, to Brentwood, California, where we were renting a house for three months while my father ship-shaped the Brentwood branch of the investment firm where he worked, telling me they needed some midwestern common sense to get that hippie-dippie office running smoothly.

I'd spent my spring imagining two versions of my summer—the one I would tell my friends, jealous of my glamorous move to California, and the one I knew would actually occur, with my mother and me bored on someone else's couch, our rabbit ears set to the games. Driving into California, crossing state line after state line from sweltering heat and humidity into sunshine and tan lines, our windows rolled down because Mom said it saved on gas, I knew I was in for the crappiest summer of my life. And to make it worse, when we returned, I'd have to lie and say how great it was, telling Shelly Fisher, my archnemesis of the fifth grade, that I'd made out with a movie star.

A few months before the games were to start, before we heard word one from the Russians about a boycott, McDonald's had unveiled their "When the U.S. Wins, You Win" campaign. Every pull-off tab had an event, and if an American won that event you'd get a prize: a Big Mac for a gold, fries for a silver, a Coke for a bronze. It wasn't as showy or sexy as their later Monopoly campaigns where the golden ticket was a million dollars, but the payout was more likely, and, to a kid, a hamburger seemed more realistic than a million bucks. I remember at the time thinking about the poor athletes, how now they'd have this added pressure of people wanting their free burgers on top of everything else, which should tell you something about my inability to understand stakes. This promotion went down in history as one of the worst marketing campaigns in the United States, an obvious and utter failure. Every McDonald's in America had drive-thrus eight cars deep, a line that extended out the door and down the block, all those people there for their free food. A McDonald's in El Segundo ran out of buns, which nearly caused a riot, the hamburger-crazed mob featured on the evening news. McDonald's ended up losing millions, and years later in a college marketing class when we studied projects and analysis, I learned that heads rolled. Even so, it was the greatest thing to ever happen in my young life: all those medals tallied into free burgers that I ate with my new best friend, Amy Silber.

Moving to a new state at the beginning of the summer had seemed like a death sentence. I wouldn't have school as an opportunity to meet new people, and my mother was not the type to pursue extra-curricular activities, so other than time at the library—a place you were not necessarily encouraged to interact and make noise—I was afraid I'd spend the summer organizing farms for my Smurfs in the backyard. But Amy lived right next door to us, across a wide swath of lawn, and in addition to being ten thousand times cooler than anyone I knew in Nebraska, she had an in-ground pool. I'd never met anyone who owned a pool before and she was generous about it, coming over the day we moved in and asking if I liked to swim. I was eleven; of course I liked to swim. Along with being the only person in California I had spoken to other than my mother, Amy was black, which seemed to have a certain amount of cachet in the early '80s. *The Cosby Show* wouldn't begin airing until that September, but I felt, as America, we were ready for the Huxtables, for an affluent black family with a funny dad who spoke in funny voices to show us they were just like white people. There were three black kids in my school back in Nebraska. It's not like I'd never known any black people, but this was the first one whose house I was in, or who I ate lunch with, or who admitted, same as me, that she was utterly in love with Ralph Macchio. When Amy came over that first day she had Magic Marker up and down her arm—a badass, preadolescent tattooing of sorts—and explained it was permanent, that her own inherent boredom would be on her skin the rest of her life. (It wouldn't be; by the time we got out of the pool that first day, the chlorine had worked its magic and faded it in half.) She also had a daring amount of eye shadow on, which I could tell made my mother suspicious.

That first afternoon our moving van was lost in traffic and delayed a few hours, and Amy asked if we wanted to come over for lunch. My mother, weary from the drive out—a three-day venture we made alone, my father already in California for his temporary position at IMV while we waited for my summer break to start—said that sounded lovely. We followed Amy over to her house where her mother was waiting, a meal already prepared by Marcia, a Hispanic woman who was the maid, nanny, and cook. I had never met anyone with help before either—a thing I thought only happened on TV—and it was like entering a foreign country, unsure how I should act or behave. My mother in particular was unnerved by all this. I remember that afternoon how she unfolded her napkin in her lap (cloth, for lunch!) then thought better of it and left it next to her plate until the meal was served.

"It's a beautiful day," Amy's mother, Mrs. Silber, had said. "Why don't we eat next to the pool?"

Marcia took our plates and utensils outside and rearranged them on the patio—what Mrs. Silber called a "lanai." We ate blueberry muffins and cantaloupe, Amy rolling her eyes, telling me her mother was always on a diet.

"Mine too!" I'd whispered back, another sign we would be best friends, never mind that every mother we knew was constantly on a diet, although Amy's was thinner than most, her arms exposed and sleek in a sleeveless blouse, my mother's covered by a three-quarter length sleeve, pasty from the Nebraska winter and the rainy spring.

Afterward, my mother clodhopped home, her feet in a pair of Dr. Scholls that left block-like indents across the lawn. I could see my father in the driveway, the moving truck next to him, our possessions being marched in three men at a time. I held up a hand to wave and he did too, although he stayed where he was standing and I walked no faster.

"A lanai," my mother said, shaking her head. "You know as well as me it's just a patio."

My father was gone a lot that summer, acclimating to his new position at IMV. He would leave me articles about goings-on about town: a new panda born at the L.A. Zoo, or a break-dancing class at the Y. He communicated with me through articles that had nothing to do with either of us, these missives he'd cut out before leaving the house in the morning, the moon still high as he drank his coffee. I'd wake in the morning well past nine and find them on the kitchen counter, or what my mother now called the counter-*top*, which is what Mrs. Silber had called it, as in, "Marcia, my hands are full watching the girls in the pool. Will you bring me that pitcher of water from the countertop?"

Looking back I can recognize now that my mother had her own problems to deal with. I wasn't sure what had prompted the move and assumed it was as cut and dried as the promotion my parents told me about, although later it was referred to as a lateral move my father had to make to keep his job, a result of affirmative action.

Mom tried to stay true to her midwestern roots and be kind to everyone, putting on a brave face as she maneuvered through traffic on the way to Vons or the drugstore for the waterproof sunblock I sorely needed. She'd be nice to the clerks, telling them she was still getting her bearings in this new city and state. As they rang a ham steak into the register, their fingernails clicking efficiently, she'd say she'd grown up on an honest-to-god hog farm in the middle of nowhere, Nebraska. She'd point to the steak and tell them that ham could be one of her pets. Sometimes they'd laugh and tell us about seeing a pig for the first time at Knott's Berry Farm or mention another rural animal—a sheep maybe—that they'd always thought was cute. More often than not though they'd ignore the comment, my mother's smile extended like a hand no one wanted to shake. When that happened, she'd get back in the car and slam the drive shaft in gear so hard the car would vibrate with her anger. One time she drove off and left me at the grocery store's entrance with our full cart, returning ten minutes later without so much as an apology.

My mother spent a lot of time in her room that summer, closeted away from me and my father, all of the rooms perfectly temperature-controlled in a house, I realized later, we couldn't afford. But what might have looked like abandonment presented itself as an opportunity—a house to myself, no parents to bug me—and I spent nearly every day at the pool next door with Amy. It was the year the Olympics added synchronized swimming as an event, which seemed like a fancy way of dancing without anyone being able to see how bad you were at it. The Silbers had the pool put in the year before, and while it wasn't Olympic size, it was certainly impressive compared to the inflatable toddler pools in the backyards of Nebraska. Amy and I convinced our mothers to buy us navy and red bathing suits—hers a red and navy striped two-piece, mine a one-piece navy with red piping—so we would have the semblance of being a team. Every day we would practice our moves in the morning, performing for our mothers in the afternoon as they lounged on lawn furniture around the cement edge. Mrs. Silber would be dressed in a tennis outfit or pedal pushers and a matching blouse, her hair soft and feathered, lipstick smoothed on her lips. My mother wore cutoff jeans and old T-shirts of my father's, grumbling every afternoon that she wasn't going to change to go to a neighbor's. "I used to go to Harriet Gunderson's in my bathrobe, for god's sake. And no one said 'boo' about it."

"That doesn't mean it was a good idea," I said.

"That woman puts on airs," she said, pointing a finger at me, referring, I assumed, to Mrs. Silber not Harriet. I didn't understand why it was an air and not Mrs. Silber's real self, when she seemed, as well as I could tell, to keep the appearance up every day. It was the first time I could remember my mother being open about disliking someone (even when the cashiers were rude to her, she'd smile as she took her change). The one saving grace was that they both liked to drink and seemed to recognize it was problematic to do so alone. They would start with that first glass together in the afternoon, which made it acceptable, Mom's sobriety staying at a slow simmer the rest of the day.

Amy and I didn't realize all this at the time, or if we did, we didn't care. We were happy to have an audience, happy our mothers let us be in the pool. We began with fairly simple routines—a lot of arm waving and collapsing underwater, complicated by some back floating and a jive routine where we'd clap our hands above our heads. We were supposed to be a team, twins of each other, but that wasn't the case. Amy wore her hair in a short afro that went from wet to dry with a flick of her head while mine would hang limply at my shoulders, drying flat and parted in the middle. She looked better in her swimsuit—her belly smooth between her swimsuit top and bottom—while Lycra hid my chubby stomach, although certainly not very well. She had a mass of friendship bracelets up her arm that she never took off and a toe ring I thought was so neat I had to remind myself not to stare. I only had four friendship bracelets, and if Amy had asked whom they were from, I would have lied and said friends in Lincoln. (My mother had braided them in the hotel on the way out.) Even though Amy was my best friend and I was insanely jealous of almost everything about her from the hair to the pool to the toe ring, a part of me knew I'd rather be me than her. We were a country ready for the Huxtables but only in the thirty-two-inch box in our living rooms, not moving next door and owning swimming pools. I never said this to Amy, not even at the end, and to the best of my memory, I never acted this way. But I thought it, I did, and I guess that says more than anything about what kind of best friend I really was.

The opening ceremonies were patriotic excess at their best, starting with the torch being run out all the way from New York. Everything was bigger and better, shinier and newer, with a soundtrack specially written for the games with songs by Foreigner and Herbie Hancock. Ronald Reagan hosted the ceremonies, and at some point, a man from the future flew in on a jetpack. It was clear, given the hoopla, that as a country the Olympics meant something to us, and as Amy and I back floated in her pool we talked about what the games might look like in 1988. If we really took our swimming seriously and practiced every day, did we think we'd get a chance to compete? It felt good to care so much about our country, and it was easy because we were winning, although many nights there were reports on the news about fights or riots, Americans jacked up on too much adrenaline. There was an anonymity and mob mentality to the fervor, an excuse to be obnoxious, and years later when our troops killed Osama bin Laden and frat boys celebrated in the street, I would have the same underlying sense of dread. How utterly shortsighted of us to not remember our slight four years ago when we boycotted the Olympics because of the Soviet invasion of Afghanistan. How could we not think that the Russians might pull a similar stunt on us? How could we not see that one action might lead to another? The only Americans upset about the whole thing ended up being the McDonald's execs who lost millions, while the rest of us were cheering, patting ourselves on the back for winning all the golds. But did it really count as winning if you bullied everyone else into not showing up?

The first day of competition, America won a slew of medals, and when we went to cash in our tickets at McDonald's we got six more tabs, five of which would be winners. We convinced one of our mothers to take us to Vons to get poster board, markers, and a ream of tape to make a chart listing all of the Olympic events. We taped the event tabs on the poster board the moment we got home, each event and day filling up, multiplying after every meal. Each area, such as water sports or gymnastics, had a column with individual rows for each event. There was a place to mark the outcome, and a place to tape our winning ticket, and sometimes we would have more than one per event. You might get three Big Macs for a wrestling event because it was a sport predicted to be swept by the Russians, and if you cashed those in with the silver in Men's Triple Jump, you'd get fries to go with your Macs. We agreed early on to pool our winnings—a Big Mac for me, meant a Big Mac for all. Like our tickets, we pooled the Sam the Eagle pins we were collecting from different venues. Amy's favorite was the one where Sam was holding the Olympic rings around a Coca-Cola, and when I saw how much she admired it, I pinned it on her shirt. "It's yours," I said. "I want you to have it."

"Are you sure?" she asked, her fingers caressing the rings. "This pin is, like, your favorite!"

It felt great to give it away, especially because she was right: it *was* my favorite. "Absolutely," I said. "You wear it," and she wrapped those thin, dark arms around me in a hug.

The Olympics ran all day except noon to three. At noon we'd slip on our red, white, and blue T-shirts and head to McDonald's for our free lunch, then practice our swimming from one to two o'clock, and then from two to three o'clock we'd watch *General Hospital*. At three we'd get back in the pool for an hour or so to practice and

watch more games, Marcia carting the kitchen TV out on an extension cord. We knew from interviews with the athletes it was important to practice as much as we could but counted on our natural
talent (Amy's more than mine) to carry us through—that and the
fact we wanted it so badly. It seemed in this economic boom that
wanting something badly might be enough.

By the time the Olympics were underway, we were experts at
our synchronized routine, making it all the way through a song
with no more than three or four mistakes, practically perfection.
Our opening moves for "Beat It" (snapping our fingers through
the water, which required a delicate balance of having your hands
far enough in the water to produce a splash, but far enough out to
make some noise) were a well-oiled machine, although I would
sometimes emerge from underwater to find myself a step behind
Amy, my arms not synchronized but a shadow-move behind, my
footing off in the pool as I lagged a beat behind her.

In the evening, during re-runs of *The A-Team* and *Remington
Steele*, we would work on our essays for the *Orange County Register*'s
essay contest for grade schoolers. We were to write on how we were
inspired by one of the Olympic athletes, thinking how great it would
be in interviews for our own 1988 Olympics to talk about these winning essays we'd written, how inspiring that would be to someone
else. I was writing on Theresa Andrews, a swimmer like myself,
who won two golds that year and gave the first one to her brother
who had been injured in a biking accident. It had been between
her and Mary Lou Retton, a girl Amy and I liked because she jux-
taposed homely with perky, snapping her arms up after the dis-
mount and making the most of those big, white teeth. (We realized,
even at eleven, this might be the hand we'd been dealt.) Amy broke
the contest's rules and didn't focus on one specific person but all
the black athletes—whom she called her brothers and sisters—
saying they were inspiring her to bigger and better things, although
what was better than a pool in your backyard I could hardly imagine. I didn't point out to her that the rules had said specifically you

needed to pick one athlete, and if I'm honest, it wasn't because I was being supportive but because I wanted to win.

Most nights we would alternate which house we slept in: one night in my house, the next in Amy's. We were best friends and when you're eleven, that means something—swapping tooth-brushes and pajamas, confessing whatever it was we had to confess at that age: I had stolen a York Peppermint Patty at a grocery store in Lincoln when I was younger; Amy had put a Magic Marker moustache on the cloth Mary doll at her Sunday school. We shared that we liked being only children, but sometimes we wished we had a sister or a brother and that maybe we could pretend that's what we were—sisters. I told Amy my secrets like a bird let loose in my chest, and most nights we'd forgo sleeping in the twin beds we both had in our rooms and fall asleep on the floor with our hands clasped between us, a spilled bowl of popcorn by our heads.

Waking in the morning at Amy's house, I'd come down to find Mrs. Silber in the kitchen, a silk towel on her head, her face drawn tight without make up, her eyes much smaller than I would have imagined as she squinted against the morning light. "Did you two have a nice night?" she'd ask, and I'd nod and flee back upstairs.

The morning was the time I really thought about the Silbers being different from us, about the Silbers being black. I never saw Mrs. Silber without lipstick even at the grocery store, while my own mother worked hard to get her hair brushed by dinnertime, but in the morning, Mrs. Silber seemed vulnerable, not yet shored up for the day. Marcia would arrive at nine, at which point Mrs. Silber would have changed into slacks neatly marked with a crease. One morning as Mrs. Silber made her slow way upstairs, I told Amy that I loved how her mom got dressed up for the day, embarrassed that my own mother still hadn't unpacked beyond what she called her gardening clothes. Amy took a bite of her peanut-butter toast, care-ful to wipe crumbs from her mouth. "Your mom's white," she said. "She can afford to be a slob," and her voicing of what made us dif-ferent felt like a slap in the face. We had worked so hard to pretend we were the same, I'd almost wondered if she were stupid enough to think we really were.

A few days after the Olympics, Amy got the call from the *Orange County Register* saying her essay hadn't won because it hadn't focused on just one athlete, but that they'd like to run it anyway, as a companion piece on what it meant to be an American. I was there when she got the call and stayed only long enough to congratulate her before running home to see if they had called me too. I waited all afternoon—this was before answering machines—and a week later got my notice of "Honorable Mention" in the mail along with every other kid who had entered. It might have been here that I began to see our divide. I was upset she had won based on something I couldn't possibly have written, although I guess that was true of all of our experiences. The day the paper came out, Mrs. Silber drove us to Vons to buy enough copies to send to all her relatives. They hadn't even run the names of the Honorable Mentions like I hoped they might, and when I got home, I threw the paper away.

The final week of summer—the day before we were to head back to Nebraska—Mrs. Silber had my mother and me over for one last lunch. I remember it was a scorcher, well over ninety-five degrees, and my mother wore shorts and a ratty T-shirt of my father's, an outfit Mrs. Silber wouldn't have been caught dead in. We ate our chicken salad and red grapes, and then Mrs. Silber set her kitchen timer to fifteen minutes, enough time, she had decided, to allow us to digest.

As soon as the timer rang we snapped on the boom box and dove in for one last routine. Amy dipped underwater in conjunction with myself, our arms in harmony, our bodies aligned. I knew if we were to continue working on our routine, maybe convincing our fathers to videotape us so we could send the tapes back and forth for a critique, we would qualify in 1988.

At the end our mothers clapped, a standing ovation. "The end of summer," Mrs. Silber said. "Can you believe it? Amy will be heading to school next week. She's going to miss having Carol as a friend."

"Carol's going to miss Amy too," my mom said and turned to Mrs. Silber. "I wish we'd taken the chance to get to know each other better. Seems silly now to have been neighbors all summer and hardly know boo about the other." She sounded sincere.

Mrs. Silber smiled behind her large sunglasses. "We should have, shouldn't we?" I looked at Amy, my heart in my throat, and Amy reached for my hand underwater, both of us sure this was the moment they'd realize what good friends they could be. Maybe we could stay, not move back to Nebraska.

And then my mother, in an uncharacteristically silly move, crossed and curled her hands under her T-shirt's hem and pulled it over her head to reveal her bra—a faded beige garment yellowing under the arms. She left on her shorts but cannonballed in, a grand finale to our show. When she emerged from the water she focused on Mrs. Silber, a grin ear to ear, Amy and I clapping, both delighted by this turn of events.

"What about it, Deb?" my mother said to Mrs. Silber, and Mrs. Silber smiled at my mom, a complicated look I couldn't read behind her glasses.

"I don't think so," she said. "I'm not much for the water."

It had been a miserable three months for my mother—ripped away from people and a life she understood, deposited in L.A. where she was too scared to leave her house for fear of being run over in the traffic. We all stood suspended in the moment, each trying to read the others' faces, the emotions stomping across my mother's face fading from glee to shame to anger.

Mom pushed over to the pool's edge, her thighs fighting against the water's resistance. She lost her footing climbing out and slipped back in, and when Mrs. Silber held out her hand to help her up, my mother pretended not to see.

"We should finish getting packed," she said, ignoring the towel Mrs. Silber held out.

"But Mom!" I whined, and my mother didn't so much as turn around to debate it as she headed toward our rented house. "Now, Carol."

"I should go," I said to Amy and when she asked if I'd be coming back, I pretended, for my mother's sake, to not hear that too.

Amy came to our door that night to give back my Sam the Eagle pin, a move than incensed me. I had given her the pin as a gesture of friendship. "You keep it," I said. "I don't really want it." I wanted it to look like charity.

We had planned to spend our last day together, but after my mother and I had left the lunch, neither Amy nor I made a move to call the other. I thought because it was Amy's mother who had been so rude it was Amy's responsibility to apologize, and every minute she didn't call or walk across the lawn just further proved I was in the right. By the time Amy showed up, I was siding with my mother that Mrs. Silber could take a flying leap.

Amy leaned against the doorframe, her thin shoulder resting against the wood as she traced the rings on the pin she had worn all summer. I never would have guessed we could have an awkward moment—us! sisters!—but here it was.

"I gotta go," I said. "We're still not done packing," and Amy nodded her head and turned to leave. She turned back as I was shutting the door. "It's her hair," Amy said. "My mom can't get her hair wet. That's why she didn't get in the pool."

I thought she meant it like all ladies would mean it, that they didn't want to mess up their hair and makeup, but I was thinking only of white women. "It doesn't matter," I said, and regretted that I'd let her keep the pin. "It's not a big deal."

Mom and I had planned to leave at daybreak the next morning, but because of complications with this or that, we didn't get on the road until nine. Even so, I didn't go over and say good-bye to Amy again, while a month earlier I couldn't imagine how I'd be able to get through our departure without tears and hysterics. In the car, my mother pulled her sunglasses from behind the visor and put them over her eyes. "You ready for this?" she asked and I nodded. I had expected her to be elated about returning and me to be devastated, but somehow we met in the middle and calmly listened to Joni Mitchell eight-tracks as we cruised into Arizona. My father joined us a week later, flying in on the red-eye, and we picked up our midwestern lives as if we'd never left. I did indeed, upon returning to Lincoln, tell Shelly Fisher about my summer in California. I never lied and said I met Ralph Macchio or even a lesser celebrity, but I was sure to bring up that my best friend had been black, cashing in, as much as I could, on the black cachet. This seemed to gain me enough popularity to ready me for middle school, and the first few weeks of classes, I'd bring up Amy as much as I could. They'd serve peas at school lunch and I'd say how much Amy loved them, or if anyone at all brought up the Olympics, I'd say how we watched every single minute. It all felt like a lie, bitter in my mouth, because even though Amy had my address and I had hers, we never once sent the other a letter. I went so far as to say Amy was going to visit us at Christmas, and when she didn't show up, Shelly said she thought the whole friendship was a lie. "I bet she's not even black," she said, and even I began to doubt she was.

A year later my dad was promoted and we moved permanently to Peoria, Illinois—a reward, my mother said, for that awful summer in California. Within a few months my mom knew all the cashier's names at her regular grocery store and the Kmart, and when we'd come up in their line they'd say, "How're you today, Joyce?" pointing out that rump roast was on sale, the two of them discussing sports at the high school—football or basketball, depending on the season. We of course didn't have a synchronized swimming team, and as I entered high school, my weight shooting up in puberty, I wouldn't have been in a swimsuit in public anyway.

Years later in my college marketing class, talking about

McDonald's big failure, it was like being transported back to that summer. All the Big Macs we ate, the routines we performed, the sleepovers we had, the charts we made. I couldn't believe I'd let that friendship slip away and had to gulp air deeply to keep from crying in class. I wasn't sure I was remembering Amy accurately—had we really been that close?

The professor finished her lecture, erasing what she'd written on the chalkboard before moving onto Burger King's "Where's Herb?" fiasco. She set the eraser down on the ledge and clapped her hands together to remove the excess dust. "It just goes to show you what public perception can do," she said. "McDonald's, for all their economic loss, came out looking like heroes—supporting the US of A, patriots to the end—but the promotion was actually built on the opposite. If they'd had any faith the Americans were going to win, they never would have run the campaign."

A Democrat in Nebraska

Sam hasn't been to a Halloween party in over twenty years, since he went as an asexual Smurf in 1978. That was a confusing time in Sam's life—the tricky period between a happy childhood and the sexually forlorn teen years—and thinking back, going as an androgynous blue midget seemed like a perfect metaphor, although he couldn't pinpoint for what. Jenny stands in front of him now dressed as Jackie Kennedy, blood smeared on the pink skirt and tailored jacket. "You don't have to go," she says again, but Sam is already dressed. The blue thrift-store suit dry-cleaned, his hair slicked back yet raised on one side where the bullet would have gone through. Jenny wanted to rent a convertible and have it chauffeured to the party—him slumped over the backseat, her climbing across the trunk to escape the horror. In the end he convinced her they couldn't afford it, and besides, all the guests would be inside.

Sam pockets the car keys and holds the door for his mourning wife, knowing he *does* have to go to the party, no matter how many times she tells him otherwise. Jenny started volunteering for the Cradberg campaign three months ago, and this is the first social engagement they've had: a Halloween party where the theme is to dress as your favorite politician. What kind of person has a favorite politician?

"You know the suck-ups in the office will go as Cradberg," she said a month ago when the invitations came out. "We can do better than that."

"What about John Hinckley?" he suggested, but she shot him a withering look that let him know she no longer found his jokes amusing.

Nelson Cradberg, the democratic senatorial hopeful, is the first to greet them at the door of the party. It is held at the campaign office, a large room that looks like it could be used to sell cars or run drugs. The desks are pushed to the side supposedly for a dance floor, leaving the large room looking empty except for orange and black streamers tacked over the red, white, and blue. "Jackie, you're aging so well," Nelson says, putting an easy arm around Jenny's back. "And John, still up and about?" He laughs loudly, his mouth puffed up like a pastry. Cradberg is dressed in the same suit he wore that day, his politician's hair wet and high off the forehead.

"Who are you supposed to be?" Sam says, and runs a hand up and down in front of Cradberg, indicating the suit.

"I guess me," Cradberg says, and laughs again. "Sondra's bringing me a jogging suit and some fries from McDonald's, but she's late." Cradberg sweeps his arms wide with his index fingers extended, kind of like Tricky Dick although Sam doubts this is intentional. "There's food there and booze there," he says, cocking his fingers to different corners of the large room. "Help yourself."

Jenny puts a hand on Nelson's arm and thanks him as Sam heads for the hors d'oeuvres. Even the food seems politically correct—bland and unobtrusive fare such as pigs in a blanket with dipping sauces for kick. Sam takes a stuffed mushroom and pops it in his mouth whole.

"Could you at least get a napkin?" Jenny says, coming up behind him a moment later. She holds one out, a smear of blood from her suit catching on the corner.

"Ask not what your husband can do for you . . ." Sam begins, but Jenny just stands there, the napkin extended.

"This is important to me," she says softly. Sam understands the magnitude of a statement like that. The gubernatorial election for Nebraska is the first thing in a year that Jenny's engaged in with anything resembling heart since they moved to Lincoln from New Hampshire. When they moved she quit her job, never got a new one, and then stopped doing simple things around the house like changing light bulbs and sheets. But she was the one who wanted to move to Nebraska to be near her folks, not him. Did he need to remind her of that? His parents lived in Delaware.

A teenager dressed as Abraham Lincoln hauls in a box of records and sets them next to a turntable. "Cradberg's nephew," Jenny whispers in Sam's ear before picking up three mushrooms and putting them on a plate and handing them to Sam.

Cradberg's wife comes through the door a few minutes later, just as the nephew begins spinning records, starting with the obvious Kool and the Gang classic "Celebration." Sam is embarrassed to see a middle-aged white guy take center stage with his arms stationed above his head in an offbeat clap, the look on his face an uncomfortable mix of vanity and embarrassment. All this state has is embarrassed-looking middle-aged white guys, and Sam isn't happy about fitting so snugly into the category.

"Sondra," Jenny says and leans in for a half-hearted hug, careful not to get any blood on her boss's wife or knock over the fries in her hand. Sondra is an impressively tall woman in a boxy purple suit that hits her calves at an unflattering angle. A too-thick blonde wig and unflattering lipstick completes the look of Hillary Clinton.

"Have you seen Nelson?" she asks Jenny.

"Last I saw, he was over by the DJ."

"I hope that man realizes dancing isn't going to win any votes."

Sam laughs and Sondra looks over at him, a smile lighting on her face.

"You must be Mr. Jenny."

"Sam," he says and holds out his hand. He doesn't want to be referred to as Mr. Jenny ever again although Jenny looks pleased with the title.

"Sam," she repeats. "It's not a very good politician's name. There's no weight or money behind it, you sound like a simpleton."

"I'm not a politician," Sam says. He pauses then adds, "Or a simpleton."

"Not now," Sondra says, "a politician anyway, but maybe someday. The way your wife's whipping my husband into shape, I'm sure she has plans of her own." Sondra smiles tersely. "She's quite an assistant."

"Actually, Mrs. Cradberg," Jenny intervenes. "I'm only a volunteer." She holds up a plate of hors d'oeuvres. "Chicken wing?" Sam snaps one off the plate and sticks the meat in his mouth, sucking it from the bone and avoiding eye contact with Jenny. She sticks an elbow in his ribs.

"Oh, don't do that," Sondra says. "Let him eat a chicken wing. Men are built for messy food." She leans toward him and feels the red plaster and ketchup oozing from the back of Sam's head, the point where the bullet exited. "Poor baby has been through enough."

Her fingers are soft and cool near the wound, and he looks up to her weathered face, surprised to see that underneath the wig and too-pale lipstick she is actually quite attractive, moreso than you'd expect for a woman with Cradberg.

Sam trails behind Jenny for the next hour, moving from table to table, morphing into the funny sidekick, the dedicated husband, the concerned voter. At each table Jenny stays consistent and Sam tells himself it's because she works with these people every day—they know her—and there is no role to play, no need to pretend. What surprises him the most is how little his reaction to their comments actually seems to matter. All the women smile at him like he is the perfect trailing spouse; the men look at him like he looked at Cradberg, surprised he could get a woman like that. What they're really interested in is Jenny. A jowly man at table number seven asks her what she thinks about the gun-control debate that has been ebbing and flowing for years and she shakes her head thoughtfully, responding with something smart-sounding Sam can hardly follow about the county-by-county vote on the senatorial floor. He knows his wife believes in politics and has been politically active on some level for her entire adult life—voting in local elections, petitioning for free recycling in New Hampshire, giving full support to the smoking ban and against global warning—but he hadn't realized how *smart* she was, and on the flip side, how dumb he is. Has she always believed this passionately?

Through the hour of circulating Jenny keeps a hand on his arm or shoulder, touching him more as if she is sensing his body heat than aware of his body. He realizes on some level she is worried about what he'll say without her watchmanship and he resents this. She knows what he's capable of if left alone—that was proven in the not-so-distant past—but now they live in Nebraska, a flyover state where you could live on ten dollars an hour and have in-laws a short, short hour away. With a hand on his arm, Jenny keeps a free eye roaming through the party, and it takes Sam until table sixteen to realize she is looking for Nelson Cradberg, now cinched in a too-small red sweat suit and a white sweatband from the nineties, the McDonald's fries long gone although he holds onto the cardboard container. Sondra stands to the side a few steps back, swirling something clear in a glass. She's the only one Sam sees with a real glass-glass, not the cheap plastic everyone tries to keep from caving against the weight of their drinks. Who believes in recycling now?

Cradberg circles back a few tables later to Jenny and Sam.

"Hidy-ho," Nelson says and Jenny smiles, her hand slipping unaware from Sam to Nelson. Sam looks down at his forearm, suddenly cold.

"Are you having fun at your party?" Jenny asks.

"Oh," Nelson says, and looks down at the empty fry container. "It's not my party, it's yours, all of you. We know what's going to happen next week, we might as well go out in style."

"We don't know!" Jenny says, and Sam's head snaps away from the DJ at the vehemence in her voice. "We won't know until the final vote is counted."

Nelson smiles wanly. "I appreciate that, Jenny, I do."

"Appreciate nothing," she says, "except the votes."

"You've got mine," Sam adds wanting to be a part of the conversation, and Jenny shoots him a look that says, *Don't state the obvious, stupid.*

Sondra finds Sam over by the DJ stand. Jenny has deserted him to look at some paperwork with Cradberg in his office, and he was hoping standing by the DJ table would provide a cover, but it's all on a laptop now, no record covers to peruse, so he has nothing to do but swirl Bud Light in a plastic cup and look useless.

"You're bored," Sondra says, and he debates about the effect of saying something without Jenny's supervision before nodding his head.

"You too?"

"To tears." She focuses her attention on the caterer as the woman refills the cracker tray.

Nelson comes into the large room from the back hallway with an attractive woman, both of them laughing, her hand on his arm. In a quick moment of clarity the woman transforms into Jenny, Sam's own wife, and he's both shocked that he didn't recognize her and desperate to see her as a different person again. Perhaps it is only the dark Jackie wig disguising her short blonde hair that threw him, but it seems more than that. She was a random woman when she entered the room, not his wife, but when he looks again, he can only see Jenny.

"They're cute together, don't you think?" Sondra says.

He has never thought of his wife as cute with anyone but him, but he has to admit there is a camaraderie between her and the older man, his shiny black hair glowing under the disco ball that revolves with a giddyap that sticks then pushes forward too forcefully at the north end of each rotation, throwing off the beat of the lights. "I don't know about cute," he says.

Sondra takes a sip of her drink then pushes a finger against her teeth, checking for lipstick. "They spend a lot of hours together. More than I spend with him myself." She laughs abruptly. "Not that I'm complaining. It might sound like I am, but I'm not."

"Are you sure?"

Sondra runs a hand over the shoulder pads in her Hillary jacket. "No."

Sam wonders if he has something to worry about. It hadn't occurred to him before, but despite the goofy side, he has to admit, Nelson is a good-looking older man and powerful in politics, as far as Nebraska goes. He stands for gun control, the rights of women, public schools. What does Sam stand for? Fantasy football?

DJ Abe Lincoln plays Bob Dylan's "Blowin' In the Wind" next, a song that is terminally undanceable but that the eighteen-year-old recognizes as "political," something the old-folk Democrats might appreciate. He's sadly right, and the dance floor fills up with mismatched couples dressed like Geraldine Ferraro and Teddy Roosevelt, swaying to a beat that swept them up forty years ago. Toward the end of the song, the hall erupts in applause as Nelson Cradberg takes the stage, a wireless microphone in his hand. He snaps it on with a whirling wheeze and taps the end with a finger. "Hillary, you think you could come up here and help me?" he says and there is polite laughter.

Sondra comes up behind him and leans into the microphone. "Good thing he didn't ask for Monica," she says, and the laughter is more genuine.

Nelson takes his wife's hand and looks at her with obvious

affection. It seems to Sam as genuine an emotion as he hopes to see, but he wonders if this is a look that Cradberg's been cultivating for years, since his feet first hit the campaign trail. He remembers the frail way he and Jenny treated each other after his affair. As if it were normal for him to fetch her coffee in the morning, normal for her to cry herself to sleep. He wanted so badly to cover it all up with politeness, to smear on the affection until it took and became genuine. When she announced she was moving back home to Nebraska and he was invited if he wanted to come, how could he say anything but yes? It has become evident over the last twelve months that this was a mistake, a horrible one, but he doesn't regret saying yes. At the time it was the only answer he was able to give and the only one she could stand to hear.

The microphone whines again and Cradberg's head snaps back so quickly, a "Shit!" escaping his lips. Sam realizes Nelson has nothing as cultivated as a political image, that the Nelson Cradberg you see is the real deal. Cradberg touches the microphone again, more tentatively this time, then grins an aw-shucks grin. "Sorry about the expletive, my wife's been teaching me Republican words." The crowd laughs loudly. Up there with Sondra, they love him now, their grassroots senator and his dependable wife. "I appreciate so many of you giving up your Halloween for this," he says. "And for giving me your all in this election." He points a finger at the audience and begins counting. "Eighteen, nineteen, twenty. Well, at least I know I can count on about two dozen votes." The audience giggles nervously; some jokes are too true to be funny.

Jenny grips Sam's arm and twists the elbow on his suit. He looks at her, but she is staring at Cradberg. "It's too bad," she whispers. "He'd make a wonderful senator." Sam looks closely at his wife's face.

Sondra exits and Cradberg continues for a few more minutes— singling out the campaign manager with a twenty-five dollar gift certificate to T.G.I. Fridays and a T-shirt on gun control, and some other members of his staff. "Last but not least," he begins and

Jenny smiles, smoothing the blood spatter on her skirt. "I want to say a special thanks to Jenny Carlisle for everything she's done for this campaign. She's mailed mailers, talked to voters, gathered signatures for petitions. She even matched my ties to my suits." There's more laughter, but Jenny appears transfixed by only the sound of Cradberg's voice as she stares at his face with unadulterated affection. "I'm sorry, Jenny. It's because of people like you that I wanted to win this election. To give future voters the right world to live in." Jenny's hand slips from Sam's elbow as she moves toward the stage, and he feels as if he's been sucker punched.

"Wait!" Sam says, and it's not until Jenny turns around that he realizes he's spoken aloud.

"Yes?" Cradberg says into the microphone.

"Just wait a minute," Sam stalls.

Jenny stops and glances from the audience to him, the smile frozen on her face. "What are you doing?" she hisses through her wide lips, but under the anger there is something else: curiosity, maybe hope. He thinks of how she watched him as they moved from table to table earlier in the night, careful of his actions and voice. That's gone now, replaced by her wonder at what he's going to say next. If only he knew.

"Let's get you up here where people can hear you, Sam," Nelson says and holds out the microphone.

Sam walks toward the stage slowly, a white, plastic keg cup flattened in his hand like a small and broken accordion. He takes the microphone. "It's just that," he starts. The crowd stares at him, and from it Jenny crystallizes as a clear and singular woman. Her pink suit, the smear of blood. The thick brunette wig with the flip at the end, lopsided now and leaning to the left. "It's just that Jenny's right. We can't count the election lost until the final vote is counted." Nelson shakes his head, his neck warbly and loose in the unzipped collar of the too-tight sweat suit. "Now Nelson," Sam continues. "Did you think there was a chance Clinton would continue his presidency after an impeachment? That . . ." He struggles for another political analogy but none comes. "Don't you have a dream? About you and your Republican brothers walking hand in hand. Who says that can't come true?"

"I'm not going to win," Cradberg says and smiles matter-of-factly at Sam then out at the crowd. "The election? I don't have a chance. What's more or less hopeful than a Democrat running in Nebraska?" The crowd stops, unsure how to continue with such a petulant leader. They're used to these speeches going a certain way with a certain energy, and now they're thrown off track. A woman in the back boos and then another boo comes from out by the restrooms.

"Oh, I don't know," Sam says, holding up his hand to ward off the groans, the microphone warming in his hand. "A man on the moon? Peace on earth? Anything's possible. There's a chance any of us could pull off something extraordinary."

Cradberg slopes him a smile. "What gives you the impression politics is extraordinary? Where did you ever come up with that?"

Sam claps the old man on the back and looks out at Jenny. "I'm an optimist, Nelson. I never would have guessed it myself, but it's true."

"That's a sad way to go through life."

Jenny smiles at him, her eyes like wet crystals.

"Tell me about it," Sam says. "But if *you* don't think you'll win, who else will?" Sam pulls Nelson closer in a one-armed hug, and because curiosity is too much, swipes a hand through the old man's hair. It's not wet at all, but surprisingly soft, the shine coming from the deep blue-black color, like a Labrador retriever's coat. It must be dyed, which makes Sam both relieved and sad. "Is there any chance—even the slightest—that you could win next Tuesday?"

"The slightest?" Cradberg repeats, and the crowd begins a steady clap, gathering momentum from different edges of the room. They've decided now that this is planned—like good cop–bad cop.

"The slightest," Sam says, and holds his finger and thumb close together above Cradberg's shoulder showing the smallest space.

Maybe Jenny did sleep with Cradberg, maybe not. Who's to say she wouldn't be justified.

"I guess there's the *slightest*," Cradberg says, and the audience breaks out in erratic applause, Jenny toward the front of the pack clapping and smiling at Sam, her eyes not swinging to Nelson. They continue clapping as if he's announced his victory, and as if the record were ready the whole time, planned on the agenda, Abe Lincoln starts the opening chords of Queen's "We Are the Champions." At eighteen, the boy is so clueless about Nebraska politics he assumed this would be the right song all along.

Sam exits the small stage to a louder burst of applause, handing the microphone to Sondra as she climbs the stairs to lend support to her husband. On the floor Sam puts an arm around his own wife, waving to the audience like the politician he's become. "He doesn't stand a chance," Jenny says, smiling at Sam.

"Listen to my speech," he whispers. "That isn't always the point."

The Only Thing That Can Take You

The sun crept an hour higher in the sky before a pickup finally pulled to the side of the interstate to save us. The driver cocked his elbow out the window in a flannel shirt with the sleeves ripped off, and as he threw the gearshift to park I saw his face in the side mirror as a mass of veins. I realized later the glass was merely broken.

"You need help," he said, not asking a question as he popped out of the cab and walked toward us. Marshall stood to offer his hand, and I saw the man was much shorter than I'd thought seeing his arm slung out the cab window, shorter even than Marshall.

"Seems to be car trouble," Marshall said and pointed to the raised hood as he spanked the dust off the seat of his khaki pants. The air-conditioning went kaput two weeks ago in the Jetta, and I knew that should have been the first clue something was wrong. Now we were stranded an inch into the Nebraska map, the heat bearing down like a physical thing.

The man stared at Marshall. "I assumed that," he said, then spread his arms and set his palms on the grill of the car, leaning in. "When's the last time you flushed the exhaust?"

Marshall put a hand on his hip and looked at the baking horizon. "Year ago?" he said.

"There's no such thing as flushing the exhaust," the man said. "I just wondered what kind of a guy I was dealing with."

I laughed and Marshall shot me a look. "Can you see what the trouble is?" Marshall asked.

The man rattled his knuckles against the engine before stretching his arms behind his back, his chest expanding. "Whatever it is, you're not going to be driving this tonight." He held out a greasy hand to Marshall. "I'm Bill."

"Marshall," Marshall said and shook his hand. "This is my wife, Deb." I held out my hand but Bill turned away and buried his face back in the engine.

"I'm heading to town if you want a ride. Can call a tow truck too if you want to take it to the garage. I should warn you, though, not much chance of getting foreign car parts here on a Sunday if you need them."

Marshall began to laugh his horsy laugh, then stopped when he looked at Bill's face. "You're serious? It's a Volkswagen. We need to be in Lincoln by tomorrow morning."

"Not much chance of getting a taxi either." He pulled the hood arm down and the hood slammed like a gunshot. "Like I said, I can take you to Hubert where you can get a hotel room, but you're not getting much further tonight."

"We appreciate that," I said but Bill still wouldn't look at me, only at Marshall.

Resigned, Marshall said, "A ride would be great, thanks." He opened the trunk and got our overnight bags while I grabbed my purse and locked the doors.

"Good thing you locked it," Bill said, surprising me when I turned around by looking directly at me.

"Why's that?"

"I'm joking," he said. "It was a joke. No one's going to steal a broken car except for parts, which they'd break a window for."

"That's reassuring."

"Wasn't meant to be." There was something about Bill that made me like him despite my better instincts. "You should leave the doors unlocked, it's a show of good faith," and I did.

The smell of smoke and gas were strong in Bill's pickup. Faded plastic cups lined the floors and the ashtray overflowed with butts, spilling ashes to the mats and carpet. He tapped a finger on the A/C panel. "Sorry. Busted." We rode in silence ten miles or so, the wind whipping our hair, a rustling white noise. We were squeezed in a small space in the cab of the pickup, our thighs all touching, mine in shorts next to Bill's denimed leg. Marshall, uncomfortable with no one talking, asked if there was anywhere good to eat in town.

"Raffie's got a good steak," Bill said. He looked at me for the second time. "I suppose you're a vegetarian." There was nothing spectacular about Bill's eyes—a brownish hazel, average sized. I noted this as something of a disappointment.

"No," I said. "I eat meat." Marshall and I had tried vegetarianism a few years ago for a summer but it had left me weak, craving meat until I'd finally pulled into a diner off Lake Street and ordered a rare burger to go, the pink juices running to my chin as I ate it in the car.

Bill asked what we were doing near Hubert, and Marshall told him about the job interviews we had in Lincoln—him for a hospital administrator position at Bryan, mine at the Sheldon Gallery as assistant curator. I stared out the smudged windshield. We didn't have aggressive flatness like this in Colorado, a landscape where hills grew out of mountains and fed into houses and towns. Here in Nebraska there was nothing. Just a chance to get out of debt and become Cornhuskers.

Bill shifted his short legs further back on the seat as he sat up straighter. "You know a lot about art?" he said to me.

I smiled demurely. "I know a bit."

Marshall poked his head forward and looked at Bill. "She went to Colorado State for art and art history, she's a walking encyclopedia. She should be running a gallery not fetching coffee."

"I work at a coffee shop," I said, "but I do more than fetch coffee." It was a temporary job I started three years ago after grad school, the only job my degree would quality me for. "I'm interviewing for a job at the Sheldon. Assistant curator."

"That's great," Bill said. "I'm kind of an artist myself." I thought of my canvases at home, the natural light flowing from a skylight we'd soon abandon.

I smiled at Bill like I had learned in art school. "That's great," I shouted, the dusty, thick breeze blowing through the cab, lifting my hair off my face before it settled back down, hotter and heavier than before. "Everyone should have a way of expressing themselves. Really, that's great."

Bill dropped us at a local motel a mile off the interstate where we charged the room, Marshall's fingers strumming the countertops like nervous mice, waiting to see if the card would go through. We walked across the concrete parking lot to our room, and as Marshall unlocked the door, another wave of heat hit from inside.

"Fuck," he said, and shoved his suitcase to the floor. I fell on the slick bed, my back sticking slightly as Marshall rattled the knobs on the air conditioner. "What now?" he asked. "We've got to be in Lincoln tomorrow and we've got no car. No air. Nothing." The bedspread underneath me was an assault of pink and green florals with curtains to match; they looked like large beds themselves, leaned up against the wall.

"Thanks for the recap. If you start walking now . . ."

"That's not funny, Deb. You know I don't think that's funny." Marshall called the front office but got a busy signal. He rummaged in his suitcase for his Dopp kit then flipped on the TV and leaned into the mirror to take out his contacts, poking an angry finger in his eye. "Fuck," he said again, more emphatically this time.

I went to the bathroom to wash the grime from my face and neck. In the tiny metal wastebasket hidden behind the toilet was a bloody sanitary napkin unfolding like a fist from its toilet paper wrapper. I lunged toward the toilet, my stomach convulsing as Marshall knocked once on the door. "What're we going to do about dinner?

Where do you want to eat?" I pulled a Kleenex from the box and let it fall in the wastebasket, not waiting to see if it stained red, how fresh the blood might actually be.

"I'm not hungry," I said as I came out, the trail mix from earlier revolving in my stomach. "This place is disgusting, I don't want to sleep here."

Marshall opened nightstand drawers looking for a phone book but found only a gold-covered Gideon's Bible. He slammed the last drawer shut. "Two weeks without air-conditioning in the car and it never occurred to you to stop at a garage?"

"Nope," I said, and flopped back on the bed. I used to spend hours dissecting the hostility in Marshall's comments but now they bounced off my skin. They were no more than comments, as if he was talking to no one but himself.

The phone rang and Marshall looked at me, a blank expression on his face. "The front desk?"

"Maybe it's the new-car fairy." I leaned across the polyester-shiny bed—"or the new-wife"—and picked up the receiver. "Hello?"

I heard a man cough, then, "Can I speak to Marsh?"

I held out the phone. "Marsh?" No one called my husband anything but Marshall.

Marsh said, "Yes?" then listened for a moment. "That's awfully nice, but we figured we'd just get a pizza . . . Well, we're not very hungry." He leaned against the wall and crossed his arms. "The mechanic?" He finished the conversation and hung up the phone, sitting on the bed. "It was Bill. He wants to take us to dinner in town. He said he wants to go dutch."

"You've got to be kidding."

He lay on the bed by me, staring at the ceiling, an arm cocked under his head. "There's no delivery around here unless we want to get a sandwich from the vending machine and warm it up on the concrete out front. And besides, he said the mechanic usually goes out on Sunday nights, that there's a good chance we'll see him at dinner."

I pictured the maxi-pad in the wastebasket and knew I wouldn't eat from a vending machine at this motel.

"He's bringing his wife. It'll be a little dinner party," Marshall said, trying to lighten the mood.

I could picture her: the short skirt, the scabby knees, her hair an unnatural hue. I hated being so judgmental but I was hot and unhappy and traveling with a man who was blaming me for ruining our chances of moving to Nebraska—*Nebraska!*—not caring that Colorado, the land of mountains, was getting smaller in the rearview mirror.

"They'll have air at the restaurant," he said, his voice flat and tired. "I'm sorry, Deb, but it's the only option. We need dinner. We need a mechanic. We need a ride to town to get both, so just deal with it."

I frowned at Marshall. "You need a drink."

There was a knock on the door. "Already?" I asked, and grabbed my cosmetics bag and headed to the bathroom, avoiding the wastebasket. As I smeared powder across my chin and forehead I heard the door open, Marshall's voice and Bill's deeper voice in response. I came out a moment later and found Bill sitting on our bed, his arms splayed back as he leaned on his hands, his feet tapping on the carpet.

"Ready?" he said, then looked at Marshall. "Thought we'd go to Raffie's."

"I thought your wife was coming," I said.

"She's in the truck."

"It must be a hundred degrees out there."

"She's cold-blooded," Bill said, and winked at Marshall.

Outside, Bill pointed down the row of rooms to his pickup, one of three in the parking lot. A woman hunched at the shoulders hung out the driver's side window. "It's hot in here," she yelled.

"Oh, you're fine," Bill said. "She's my wife," he explained, but then stopped short of introductions. She was much as I expected only with large, open eyes, like a child's superimposed on an adult's face.

"I'm Linda," she said, and held a hand out the window to me. We shook and Linda opened the door and scooted over so Marshall and I could climb in. "Here," Linda said as she squeezed to the passenger door and lifted her butt in the air to wave Marshall under her with a hand. She fell back on his lap. "That's better." She was a petite thing, probably no more than five feet, and looked even shorter stooped on Marshall's lap, her tiny feet dangling in clunky black sandals, her hair large and platinum, held back in a butterfly barrette.

Bill drove to town, above the speed limit but in control. "We're glad you were free for dinner tonight," Linda said. "We haven't been out in *ages*."

"We're hoping to meet the mechanic," Marshall said, and Linda laughed delightedly.

"You already have," she said. Marshall cocked his head, and she pointed a thin, short finger to Bill who grinned and shrugged.

"Told you he'd be at Raffie's tonight."

He cruised the truck down two more streets and pulled into a parking lot across from a large brick building with a small neon sign in the window that read "Food." Inside, the restaurant was not so much a restaurant but a bar with a few booths to the side and numerous tables. The A/C was cranked so cold it was like entering a meat locker, our first break from the heat in hours. To my right was a half-skinned wildcat lunging toward me, his lips curled back, one paw in the air, ready to pounce. I screamed once and put a hand to my mouth, backing against Bill's chest.

He laughed and rapped his knuckles on the giant cat. "Don't worry, it happens to all the first-timers. Raff always puts his latest conquest toward the front so everyone knows what he's been up to."

I looked around. All the walls were covered with dead animals—

there was a full rattler pinned to the wall; a beaver sat on the end of the bar with his teeth bared and claws extended, the flat slap of his tail resting near a basket of matches. Above the doorframe there was a deer that had lost a shiny black eye and the hole, hollowed out and deep, stared back at us, t he hair underneath smoothed with grease.

"My god," I said then laughed at my own surprise. "It's a lot of animals."

"Most of them were shot by Raff himself," Linda said and pointed at a snakeskin at least six feet long on the south wall. "See that? Raff says that one bit him but he lived anyway. Is that possible, to get bit by a snake and live?"

I shrugged. "I suppose anything's possible."

Bill found us a table that was near the back and close to the bar. "What's everyone want to drink? And Marsh, if you say a margarita, you're buying the first round."

"A beer, I guess," Marshall said. He smiled goofily at the nickname.

"A light beer?" Bill said. "Or a real beer."

"A real one for me, a fake one for Deb."

Bill stood still for a moment, then laughed. "A fake one, that's good. You hear that, Linda?" And he made his way to the bar. I watched him lean on the counter, one arm swaying against the brass bar as he waited for his order.

"I just wanted water," I said to Marsh, and he snorted, knowing a light beer was what I'd planned on ordering. You don't spend four years together and not know how to order for each other.

"Trust me. I'm not the only one here who needs a drink."

Bill came back a moment later carrying the four bottles of beer efficiently between his two massive hands. I couldn't imagine he'd let a car break down in the middle of anywhere, or if he did, at least he'd be able to fix it. Marshall reached up with both hands to take his bottle.

A waitress named Jenna came over in a red half-shirt and Levis and set the thin edge of her tray on the table, leaning in. Linda straightened a bit and crossed her arms. "What can I get you guys?"

"We haven't had a chance to look at the menu yet," Marshall said and Bill laughed.

"You don't need a menu at Raffie's. You want a steak."

"But—"

Bill held a hand up to stop Marshall and nodded at Jenna. "Four steaks, medium rare." He looked around the table. "Do you want baked potatoes or fries?"

"I don't know," Marshall said. "You tell me."

Bill patted the skin on my leg in a loud harmless slap, drawing Linda's attention to the touch as I tensed, surprised more than anything else. "Whatever you want."

"Baked potato, butter on the side, please," Marshall said. "For my wife too." I clamped my mouth shut, Marshall's chest puffed out nearly as big as Bill's.

Jenna wrote this down. "And you?" she asked Linda without looking up.

"Fries."

Marshall turned to Bill. "Now about those car parts. I know you said next week, but we really do need to be in Lincoln by tomorrow."

Bill took a long drink from his beer. "Can't a man have a beer?" he asked us. "We'll talk about it after dinner. It's under control."

"Under control how?"

Linda leaned toward me and shouted a bit over the jukebox. "Around nine there's dancing. Do you like to dance?"

"What kind of dancing?"

"This kind," Linda said and shimmied her lean chest through the air. Bill laughed and took a sip of his beer.

"That's my girl."

Linda scowled at him. "One of them."

Bill leaned across the table, his hand slipping from my knee to hers. "The best one." He looked at Marshall and me. "She's always complaining that I don't take her out for a nice dinner with couple friends, and then here I go and deliver them straight to her and she wants to make a scene."

Linda unclipped her barrette, rearranged her hair, and snapped it back into place. "I'm not making a scene. You don't know what making a scene looks like if you think this is making a scene."

Bill clapped a hand on Marshall's back and leaned in shaking his head. "Why do we do it?" he asked Marshall. "What's even the point?"

"To what?" Marshall asked, confused.

"Exactly," Bill responded.

It was 10:15 and The Boners had been playing for over an hour now, the same heavy metal Bill favored in the truck. Marshall was knocking a wrist against the side of the table in what he thought was rhythm to the song, his feet like mismatched hooves in motion under the table. He was enjoying himself in a way I found surprising and delightful, like a dog reading the paper. He appeared to have forgotten about the car and the interviews, at least momentarily, and we were veering rapidly toward enjoying ourselves.

Bill trailed a path in the sawdust with his heels on the way back from the bar. He held out a meaty hand and asked if I'd like to dance.

Out on the dance floor his hands were what I'd imagined—rough and dry—and like his eyes, disappointing in their predictability. He cleared his throat. "Listen. I just want to say I meant what I said earlier about your job sounding nice."

"My job?" I tried to remember back to the conversation in the truck. I steamed milk and poured coffee with a group of people I knew from grad school, a tip jar brimming with goodwill if not money. We knew what it meant to be unappreciated. "Oh, you mean the job I'm interviewing for?"

"I'd love it if you'd come over and look at my work." I sensed more than felt Bill pull me closer. "I know you're only passing through, but I think I'm doing something you'd really like. I think it's worth taking a look at."

"Something I'd like?" I echoed.

Linda and Marshall sidled up to us on the dance floor, her hand wrapped around his, obviously leading. "You've got moves," she said to Bill and laughed, her whole face expanding. I wondered just what it was Bill and Linda meant by "couple friends." I thought of our couple friends in Denver, JoAnn and George—JoAnn, who collected Civil War-era teacups and saucers, and George, who droned for hours about his botched orthodontic work—and put my hand over my mouth to stifle a laugh.

"What's so funny?" Bill asked.

"Oh. Nothing," I said.

"You're a giggly one. I wouldn't have guessed you were so giggly when I saw you at the side of the road."

I wondered how I must have looked there on the side of the road with the car hood up. Most likely like an uptight woman eating trail mix with her uptight husband who couldn't fix a car. But Bill must have seen more. Enough to know I'd want to come out for beers that night, that there was a daring side to me that Marshall didn't suspect. Back in art school I'd had six lovers, and despite what Marshall thought, I wasn't there to be an encyclopedia but a painter.

"Maybe I'm full of surprises," I said.

The Boners took another break and Marshall bowed awkwardly to Linda and led her off the dance floor. Bill steered me through the sawdust with his hand on the small of my back. At the table, Bill reached for his beer as Marshall looked hard at his watch as if confused by the numbers. "We should really get going. We've still got to figure out how we're going to get to Lincoln. Bill? Any suggestions?"

"I do have a truck out front," Bill said. "Why don't we talk about it more at our house. Maybe I could drive you to Lincoln in the morning."

"Say," Marshall said. "You promised something like that about coming out for dinner tonight. Now here we are, and it's nearly eleven and we've gotten nowhere."

"That was about meeting the mechanic," Bill reasoned. "And here I am. I've delivered one mechanic. What makes you think I'll not keep my promise when that's all I've done?"

I thought of going back to the hotel room—the oppressive heat, the bloody sanitary napkin in the wastebasket—and said, "We could come over for a quick drink while we figure it out." I turned to Marshall. "Another hour's not going to matter for getting us to the interviews."

"Maybe I could lend you my truck in the morning," Bill said. "Rather than driving you myself. You'll be coming back in a day or two I assume, right?"

"That'd be awful generous of you, Bill," Marshall said, then shrugged his shoulders. "I don't see what choice I have."

"Great," Bill said. "We'll talk it all over at our place." He put an arm around my shoulder, his skin warm from dancing. "You think you'll have time to look at my work?"

Linda looked at her watch. "It's getting late."

I grabbed my purse from the table and slung in on my hip. "The Sheldon's going to be acquiring local talent for an exhibit," I said. I had read this on their website. "Hubert's not that far from Lincoln."

Bill smiled and put that reassuring hand back on my lower back. "Who knows? Maybe Hubert has more to offer than you originally thought."

Bill and Linda's house was nothing like our apartment, which we rented for more money than Bill most likely made in a month and well more than we could afford. When we signed the lease I'd thought it impossible to put a price on natural light and hardwood floors, on the chair I kept in my studio for catnaps between projects, the arms of the corduroy smooth and threadbare. Bill and Linda's house had a worn-down porch in front where they stored exercise equipment, dog beds, broken-down cardboard boxes. To the left was a carton of car parts, grimy with grease and dust. "Don't mind that," Linda said, and stepped over an old garden hose, her high heels clattering on the uneven surface. "We're remodeling the basement."

Inside, the house smelled of mold and Pine Sol, and as Bill opened a bottle of whiskey, a chocolate lab mix lumbered into the kitchen and sniffed his way up Marshall's pant leg signaling in on his crotch. "What can I get you to drink?" Bill said, ignoring the dog. "We've got this or beer." In the corner of the kitchen was a defunct toilet where Linda grew geraniums, on the counter was a toaster painted with a picture of JFK's face.

"Or wine," Linda said, and smacked the dog on the nose. The dog shuffled out of the kitchen and climbed, with considerable effort, onto a chair in the living room where a coating of hair lined the cushion. "We've got red or white." She turned to Bill. "Not everyone wants to drink beer like an imbecile." She turned back to me, a hand on her heart. "We went to Denver a couple of years ago. It was beautiful."

"We really need to discuss getting us to Lincoln," Marshall said as Bill took two glasses from the cupboard.

"I'm a terrible host!" Linda said suddenly and ran to the living room to turn on the stereo, shooing a hand at the dog as she scurried past. The dog merely sneezed. I followed her into the other room, my eyes drawn instantly to a blue bike hanging from the ceiling above the couch. It was a girl's bike complete with a banana seat and baseball cards snaked in the spokes—like childhood itself, up on the wall.

"See here?" Bill said, his voice surprisingly close. He pointed to the underside of the frame. I looked closer and saw the bumps and grooves underneath numerous layers of paint. There were bends in the metal which he must have hammered out, the bumps and nicks not masked by the paint. It wasn't the normal wear and tear of a child's bike.

"Was there an accident?"

"Kid got hit by a truck over near Ogallala, she died about a week later. I was called out to tow the truck and no one thought to pick up the bike. I figured I'd better do it so the folks wouldn't have to see." I looked at Bill queerly as if seeing him for the first time. The dull-brown eyes, his calloused hands. I didn't know what to think of the bike, how different it was from what I originally expected. "The paper said she was a good kid. In the accelerated reading program at her grade school." He reached out and took my hand, his skin hot. "That's not what I want to show you. It's outside."

"Bill," Linda said, and I heard the warning in her voice. Marshall pulled on the bike's front tire and the clatter of cards filled the room.

I followed Bill to the dark backyard where he bent low near the side of the house and turned on a switch, flooding the yard with light. It took my eyes a moment to focus, and at first I merely saw a small junk car disassembled and cluttering the grass, a tarp on sticks protecting it from the elements. Bill stared at me, expecting a response. I walked into the yard and the pieces began to take form, not a car at all but many, all makes and models. The body, as far as I could tell, was Cadillac, Ford, and Hyundai, pieced together properly in places, and in others, welded messily together, the imperfections not buffed out but left like thick clots on the side of the car. The body was painted in bright rainbowlike colors, each body piece a different shade, drawing attention to the mismatched mistakes.

"Check this out," Bill said and popped the hood, which groaned in protest in the heat and humidity. Inside the parts were a shiny, uniform black; although drawn from different cars, here they became one, larger than the sum of their parts. I thought of my own work—the too-controlled colors, the uniform strokes. I hadn't painted in over a year although I visited my studio every day. The natural light, the well-worn chair—they were all I had left of the life I'd promised myself in Denver, and if we left, even the promise was gone. "Do you get it?" Bill said. "It's not a car. It's Car." He grinned wildly. "Every car I've worked on in the past six years is here, even if it's just a bolt." He leaned in the driver's window and across the leather bucket seat and the vinyl passenger seat and popped the glove box. "See this?" he said. "Look familiar?" I peered closer at the map in his hand—a thin yellow line highlighted our trip from Denver to Lincoln, circles at rest stops where we planned to stop and pee. Marshall was right: I made coffee. Nothing like a car in the backyard, hoping to run, wholly unseen before. I didn't know if Bill's car meant something or not, but it was something he had made that he believed in, which was a better description of art than anything I'd come up with. I wanted to kick the car or Bill or Marshall or myself.

I tore the map from Bill's hand and stalked toward the house. Linda was at the kitchen door with another whiskey and water in her hand, watching us.

"I'm going to bed," she said dully. "I thought we were going to have a fun night out, and it's just you in the backyard with another woman."

"Lin, wait." Bill snapped off the light, the car covered again in darkness. "She wanted to see the car," Bill pleaded. "We were only talking about the art."

"Oh, Jesus, Bill. Isn't that what they always want to talk about?"

Marshall emerged behind Linda's silhouette. "What's going on?" he asked, as Bill stumbled through the dark toward the kitchen door.

"I'm serious, baby," Bill said but Linda pushed his hand off her arm.

"All I wanted was a night out."

"We should go," I said and gathered my purse.

"Wait," Bill said. "I want to know what you think." He reached a hand for my shoulder and I slapped it away.

"Your car is stupid," I hissed at Bill, veering toward the light of the kitchen from the backyard. I grabbed Marshall by the elbow and pulled him behind me. It was the meanest thing I could think to say and wholly untrue. I knew little, but I knew that much.

Bill laughed abruptly. "When the car's up and running, see how stupid you think it is then," he said cruelly. "When you need to get somewhere and it's the only thing that can take you."

"What car?" Marshall said, but I gave his arm another tug.

Out in the driveway Marshall stopped and wouldn't walk any further. "What car, Deb? We need to take any ride we can get at this point." He looked closely at my face and in that moment Bill snapped off the outside front light leaving us in darkness. I could see him in the living room, the curtain pulled back to watch us. I had no idea the direction of our motel.

Marshall looked at his watch; it was after midnight. "We need to go back in," he said. "I'm not walking around this town all night. We need to find a ride."

But there was no way I was going back. "It's small enough we can circle out from here and find the motel. I think Raffie's is that way." I pointed left, toward what I hoped was north.

"You don't have a clue," Marshall said, and all I could do was shrug my shoulders. It was true.

"We can't go back in there," I said. "We can't go back."

"And whose fault is that?" Marshall spat, then followed it with a resigned sigh. "We're never going to make it, are we?" It took me a moment to remember what he was talking about—the interviews in Lincoln—why we were stuck in rural Nebraska in the first place. It seemed irrelevant now, as if this night was why we were really traveling.

I wiped the sweat from my face with the hem of my shirt and began walking, not stopping to see if Marshall would follow. We both knew even if we backtracked far enough, we wouldn't end up where we started. That out here in the dead of night, getting back home seemed as impossible as getting where we were going in the first place.

All I Want Is You

Toward the end of the evening, when our forks are resting on the sides of our plates and we're debating about rounding into dessert or holding off, Patty puts her hand on mine and asks me to tell the story, the one about the air band in Wisconsin in the eighties. This is Patty's favorite kind of dinner party, with four couples brought together who would never meet in real life—a high-wire act of hosting she has a unique talent for pulling off. Patty's twelve-year-old daughter, Cass, is spending the weekend with her father in Kearney, so Patty's packed a big bag and moved in with me for two days— lipstick on the bathroom counter and two coffee cups in the kitchen sink. She's invited three other couples and so far we've gotten along well, if politely, but we're entering the true test, that phase of the evening where we tell stories to define ourselves, the ones we reserve for new company because everyone who knows us has already heard them.

Barry, of the couple Nimisha and Barry, is foreman of the con- struction project that's been going on for a year on I-80, and he's already told a story about seeing a semi full of turkeys jackknife two days before Thanksgiving. The back of the truck popped open and hundreds of turkeys flew in the air, unharmed and loose with a vengeance. Rush-hour traffic was shut down for two hours, the mood on the interstate anything but convivial while highway patrol

dealt with the mess. Betsy of Claire and Betsy laughs, throwing
her whole head back. She remembers hearing the story three years
ago on the evening news. Nimisha and Barry are the only people
with children except for Patty—two under the age of three—and
they have a cell phone on the table between them, which they've
done their best to ignore. As far as I can tell, Patty met Nimisha at
the pediatrician when she took Cass for an annual physical. Pats
is not shy about talking to strangers, especially those with kids.

Ursula and C.J. are another couple. Ursula and Patty work for
the same bank but at different branches and have been friends for
years, but C.J. is new to the table. His story involved a cadaver and
a practical joke he played on someone in med school and, at best,
Patty is now skeptical of the pairing. A doctor, though. That's hard
to beat.

For all I know the last couple, Claire and Betsy, Patty met in the
grocery store picking up the last minute supplies for this dinner.

"Tell it," Patty says again. "The long version." Patty is not an
easy woman to say no to, and as usual I'm happy to oblige her. She's
the reason I have flower boxes lining the front of my house, why
we both know how to two-step. The story, the one she wants me
to tell, is about an air band I was in back in college with Kevin
Moran and Arnold Schmidt—two guys I haven't seen in over twenty
years. I've learned the right tone to tell the story: self-deprecating,
humorous, serious about the facts if not the details.

"You really want me to tell this again?" I ask and Patty claps her
hands. I know from knowing her that her ankles are crossed under
the table, that she just kicked them up a bit as she leaned forward
for the clap. Her face is pink from too much wine, her excitement
contagious.

"This I've got to hear," Claire says and Nimisha nods in agreement, pushing aside her plate and settling her elbows on the table.

The band had started on a lark. Me, Schmidty, and Kevin were sitting around listening to The Cars one night in Kev's apartment,

the second story of a house on Lafayette he rented with this pot-head named Toolie Delane. It was 1985 Milwaukee, and we were fans of The Cars but not fanatics. We were in agreement that Ric Ocasek was a cool guy—the ugly, skinny dude with a badass voice who didn't take himself too seriously—and the band's sound was something original, blending old-time guitar rock with the new synthesized sound rousting up the charts. We were cracking our way through a second twelve-pack when Schmidty told us about a flier he'd seen at Record Mania for an air-band competition that weekend down at Liquor Lyle's—ten-dollar entrance fee but a cash prize of two hundred for the winner and a small kitty for the run-ner up depending on the entrance number. I'd met Schmidty work-ing in the dorm cafeteria the year before at UW-Milwaukee when we were freshmen still living on campus, and I was impressed he was able to hit on the girls in line while wearing a hairnet. He explained that all we had to do was get up there and air guitar through a song, and we'd walk out with cash in our pockets.

"So no actual singing? No instruments?" Kev said.

Schmidty shook his head. "Just free cash."

Kev took a nervous drink of beer. "'Cause I can't sing worth shit."

"Not a problem. All you got to do is pretend to play, pretend to sing, and then watch the chicks rush the stage."

Social-wise, I had been in a slump for some time and would have agreed to anything on a Saturday night. My girlfriend, Katie, had broken up with me two and a half months earlier. We were high school sweethearts determined to give it a go at college, and we'd lasted through freshman year by the skin of our teeth, reuniting at home for the summer—her working again at the Dairy Queen while I helped my dad out at the golf course. It was like old times, like being back in high school, but by the beginning of sophomore year it became apparent I was the only one who saw that as a good thing. Riding around that summer in a caged-in golf cart, getting pelted by errant driving range balls, was a life I could have lived forever if it meant Katie by my side.

We decided that at six-one, 135 pounds, I should be Ric Ocasek. Even now, telling the story twenty-some years later, the couples at the table nod their heads, seeing the resemblance. I'm not as skinny as I used to be, but I still have the long anemic look of a man who isn't that fond of food. That night in Kev's apartment, we cleared away the coffee table and kicked the empty cans to the side. Toolie was home by now, sitting on the couch, his knees splayed and a roach in his hand. I stood a foot or so in front of Schmidty and Kev and tried my best to remember how Ocasek moved from the countless hours I'd spent on a beanbag in front of MTV, drowning my sorrows over Katie. Lucky for me, Ric Ocasek was too cool for a lot of dancing, and I mainly stood there, my hand in the air wrapped around a spatula.

Toolie nodded his head to the song, and at the end held up his lighter, the flame lit. "Awesome," he said, and we took his favor to heart. The next afternoon Schmidty called to tell us he'd fronted the money himself for the entrance fee, he had that much faith after one practice. "I called us The Carz, with a 'z.' Get it?"

By Thursday I'd begun to imagine the humiliation of getting up there and fake-singing a song in front of a live audience. I'd bombed out on a presentation on Thoreau in my Early American Lit class and didn't think I could handle more of that humiliation— the heart palpitations, the sweaty back, how the girl in the front row who looked critically at everyone contorted her face in pity. I asked Schmidty and Kev over beers that night if they thought we should practice. "You need to practice this?" Schmidty said and held his right arm crooked at the elbow strumming at his belt buckle, the left hand pushing strings pointlessly in the air. "You don't think you can get up and wing that?" Saturday afternoon I took the only tie I owned—a black and white striped—and colored in the lines with a Sharpie, cutting the sides to make it skinny like Ocasek's. We met up early at Lyle's for a few beers to loosen us up and to check out the competition. There were the predictable two sets of men dressed in white short-shorts, headbands, and neon sweatshirts with the sleeves cut off, their feathered hair streaked with blond; numerous girls wore fingerless lace gloves and crucifixes, their prom dresses ripped to the tulle underneath. A pudgy, bald man in a tan suit with a curlicue of hair drawn onto his forehead played air piano on the bar. Looking around, I knew we were sunk.

"Do you see now why maybe we should have practiced?" I said. "Jesus, we're going to look like fools."

"Calm down," Schmidty said. "The bartender likes the band. We've already made back the entrance fee in beer. You don't see David Lee Roth getting that kind of star treatment, do you?"

We did have coolness on our side. Even though The Cars were buzzing up the charts they weren't hitting number one, and as a band in the seventies, they had paid their dues. They were like The Boss in that way, Top Forty with integrity.

Our band wasn't up until after eleven o'clock by which time Schmidty, Kev, and I had both drank about seven beers each. David Lee Roth hadn't even bothered to lip sync "California Girls" but just danced between the bikini backups who, despite seeming nervous at the beginning, warmed to the crowd, one going so far as to push her breasts up with her hands and kiss them. I no longer cared if I looked like an idiot. A girl I didn't know had sent me over a kamikaze, thinking I was in the band, a real band I guessed. At 11:30 we took the stage. I was wearing sunglasses, my heart pounding, but looking out at the crowd it was like a cool breeze passed over me. Sounds dimmed while colors became brighter. The girl who sent me the shot was in the third row, a coy look on her face. The bouncing cords of "You Might Think" started up from the speakers as we formalized our places: Schmidty behind the set of drums the bar provided and Kev to my right holding a cardboard bass guitar constructed from twelve-packs that he'd made while we waited, nervous his body would betray him and he'd get a boner onstage.

Looking back, I can see now we were naturals. We played to the crowd but not too much, keeping the ironic distance so key to The Cars. I kept my rocker stance through most of the song—my skinny legs spread wide, one knee bopping—touching the empty micro-phone stand occasionally and only making superfluous hand move-ments when the music moved me to, just like Ric Ocasek. As a band we were contained, together, and it was obvious from the crowd's reaction—the drunken hoots, the caterwauling—that we were good. When we air-strummed to the end I tweaked the edge of my sunglasses like Ocasek did in the video, expecting my head to empty in a rush of water. On the stage that night, the move made sense to me, and I felt as wise and old as Ocasek looked.

The crowd went crazy but we kept it together long enough to get offstage. We ended up getting second place to USA for Africa, a schmaltzy choice we felt won for the sheer number of people onstage and the message of "We Are the World," which was no way to judge an air-band competition. Kev leaned his cardboard guitar against the side of the stage and chatted up Phil Collins, a guy who said he'd been doing these competitions in the Milwaukee area for the past six months and that we were one of the best he'd seen. "You should keep at it," he said. "Hone the craft." He gave us a flier for another competition Thursday night down on Waterveleit. Schmidty questioned his motives—why he'd be inter-ested in competing against us if we were so good—and he shrugged, saying if he was playing a middle-aged bald man to a pack of twenty-year-olds, he was sunk already. He did it for the thrill of getting onstage, not because he thought he would win. I was nine-teen, dumped by the only girl I'd ever loved, and I knew what he was talking about. Onstage I had felt miles away from my troubles, miles away from who I was, and when my head emptied out it was like I was seeing the world in its purest form, a smoke-filled bar full of drunk college students ready to believe in anything.

"I'm in," I said and Schmidty took the flier, folded it in his pocket, and said we'd see him there.

There's usually a lot of backtracking in the story—information to fill in, facts to check. Nimisha questions whether we'd be able to bring cardboard guitars onstage, and I explain that with air bands you were allowed instruments out of cardboard or wood and that most venues provided a drum set and microphone stand. It wasn't like air guitar which is more openly ironic, a person curling their hand at their crotch and biting their bottom lip as they overplay an invisible guitar, aware of looking like an idiot but that being part of the point. With air bands we wanted to create the illusion of being the actual band, and while no one ever admitted it, the audience wanted it too. This was Milwaukee, Wisconsin, in the 1980s, when the industrial base was headed in the toilet. Pabst, Schlitz, Harley-Davidson, Briggs and Stratton: all those companies were going through layoffs, and while the rest of America was lighting logs in the fireplace with hundred-dollar bills, we were drinking Old Mill and driving our jalopies to our convenience-store jobs, a town perpetually in recession in an age of greed. I was the first person in my family to go to college after my sister, the front-runner, ended up pregnant her junior year of high school. My dad was an assistant groundskeeper at a golf course where he didn't have a decent enough pair of shoes to wear in the clubhouse; my mom wrestled kids for a buck an hour in an unlicensed daycare out of our house, work that aged her visibly each day. Air bands were cheaper than cover bands, and real bands were out of the question. So the point, unlike with air guitar, was to make the experience as genuine as we could.

Claire and I are about the same age and she says she doesn't remember such a thing, and I know—although I'm too polite to point it out—it's because she was seeing real bands like Kool and the Gang and REO Speedwagon at coliseums and outdoor pavilions, not spending her time at dollar-pitcher bars with kids lip synching onstage.

Patty, though. Patty gets it.

The first gig we won was on New Year's Eve. I was back at my parents' in South Side for Christmas break—Schmidty and Kev holed up with their own folks in Granville and Jackson Park—and I spent hours practicing my solitary moves in front of my mom's full-length mirror knowing Katie was only six blocks away. I'd run into her at the golf course, where my dad got me a job in the restaurant making club sandwiches for retired men who were waiting for the snow to melt. It had never made sense to me why golfers lived in Wisconsin—all that waiting for the payoff of a short summer—but I understood their longing now, passing each day hoping Katie would stop by and tell me she still cared. Christmas night I stayed up watching Sylvester Stallone movies on my folk's new VCR, convinced she would show up on my doorstep—repentant, still in love, nervous I'd say no when she asked me back. In the morning my mom made waffles with her new waffle iron, another sad appliance my father had bought her on December 23rd, while my mom had been plotting his gifts since mid-August.

The day before New Year's Eve, Schmidty tracked down my folks' number and called me at home, asking my dad for Ric Ocasek. "Listen," Schmidty said, when my father finally, suspiciously, handed me the phone. "I've got a gig for us tomorrow night, at the downtown Hilton. Pot's three hundred minimum. You in or are you in?" He'd checked the bylaws and secured a fog machine for the performance. I knew if I didn't agree he'd show up anyway and terrorize me and my parents, and if I was wrong about that, my own patheticness would get the best of me and by midnight I'd be clutching the South Side Rams T-shirt Katie had left behind, wondering who she was kissing as the ball dropped, my heart in my stomach.

Schmidty and Kev showed up the next night already a few beers into the evening. That afternoon I'd exchanged the corduroys I'd gotten for Christmas for a pair of black jeans at Sears and asked my sister if I could borrow the black leather bomber jacket with shoulder pads she'd gotten from her boyfriend. My mother answered the door, telling the guys she was delighted to meet some of my college friends, still surprised her boy was so grown up. Even though Kev and Schmidty came from neighborhoods and families similar to mine, my mom had put on a dress and pantyhose. Kev and Schmidty had stepped up their game too. Schmidty wore a ripped Jack Daniels T-shirt with matching bandanas tied around his left ankle and head, and Kev was in a similar outfit but still looked like an accountant with his sloping shoulders and bowl haircut, a fitting look for guitarist Elliot Easton. The overhead light caught a sparkle on Schmidty's left ear and I saw a tiny diamond stud through the lobe, the skin around it puffed with infection. "You coming to the show?" he asked my mom, leaning in closer than was appropriate. She sniffed his breath and caught sight of his ear, a hand at her throat as she leaned back. "I'm afraid I already have plans."

"Your loss," Schmidty said and gave a wink, which my mom followed with a tiny giggle.

The hatchback of Kev's Plymouth Horizon was filled with the fog machine and new cardboard guitars he'd cut from a washing-machine box at his father's appliance store, the strings painted on with a delicate hand. In the month or so since our first gig at Liquor Lyle's we'd played in two other competitions, always placing second, but we'd succumbed to our rock-star egos, swaggering into the hotel lobby with purpose and scorn, Schmidty and me with fresh beers in our hands. We made our way to the ballroom in back where the other bands were waiting. The crowd was already revved up on wine coolers and endless keg beer, Prince's "1999" blaring from the speakers in the grand ballroom with drunk frat boys singing falsetto to the song.

We hit the stage late in the game, past the midevening slump, when the crowd was gearing up for the last half hour before the ball dropped. Stepping in front of the microphone, I felt again that moment of calm. This crowd was larger than our other shows, the room vaster, and I could see out to the sea of people, their expectant faces, everyone determined eighty-six would be their year. As Kev strummed in on the first notes of "You Might Think," and

Schmidt made an un-Schmidty like twirl of the knitting needles in his hand, I knew we'd entered a new phase in our air band, a new sense of who we were and who we pretended to be.

That night the three of us—with hundred dollar bills in our pockets after we cashed the winning check at the hotel's front desk—each ponied up thirty dollars for a room and asked the ballroom back to our suite for an after-hour's. We lifted the double beds and leaned them against the wall making more room to dance, and Schmidty and I made numerous trips to the ice machine to fill the bathtub. We were smart enough to invite the bartender who—only working through the holiday rush and not caring if he got fired—brought a half-full keg and any open liquor bottles.

There was a girl in the bathroom wearing a Lycra mini-skirt and mesh top with a visible black bra underneath. I'd seen her both before and after we performed—the first time her looking away, the second making eye contact. I had Kev pump a beer from the keg as he sat on the toilet lid, the bartender leaning against the sink, clearly drunk, telling us about the time he saw Wham! in concert. "A pack of douches," he said. "First-class homos." I brought the beer to the girl, handing it over without a word. She took a long drink and asked me where I learned to dance like that. Like what, I wondered. Ric Ocasek barely moved onstage and neither did I, but I realized it was the aura not the movement that had caught her. I shrugged and told her it was just who I was, a guy who could move. It was stupid but it worked, and later I was moving over her, then under her, the first girl since Katie. A part of me was sad that it wasn't Katie, but another part of me knew it wasn't me either.

When I tell the story I never say that I slept with the girl; I'm not that tacky, and for the reasons I'm telling the story, it's beside the point. I don't say that in a whiskey-fueled confession months later Kevin told me he'd kissed the bartender, and because I was stupid and twenty and it was the eighties, I said, "Jesus Christ, you mean you're a fag?" Instead I tell how the next morning hotel management showed up with security, twenty hungover bodies sprawled on our floor. Schmidty answered the door in a hotel towel and eyeliner, and we were charged over five hundred dollars in damages, most of it related to the wallpaper and an issue with the fog machine. Schmidt gave them a fake name and address to send us the bill, and I never told him, although I do in the story now, that it took me almost three years at fifteen dollars a month to pay off the debt we accrued.

In the New Year we started combing the underground papers and checking out fliers at the bar scene to see what air-band competitions were coming up. In Wisconsin you couldn't throw an air guitar thirty feet without hitting a college campus, and we usually didn't have more than a hundred miles to drive before we'd find drunk college kids dancing on a sticky floor, waiting for us to entertain them. Over the next few months we played at local bars, Greek fundraisers, dorm competitions, and in chilly early March, a street-band competition. The Cars continued to climb with hit after hit, and fans were buying the album now instead of relying only on the radio, and we pulled off B sides like "Stranger Eyes" and "Heartbeat City." We'd recruited two new members to fill out the band, even though it cut into our profit margin: David Gorski and Pauly Bartock, two guys I met in my poli-sci class who had performed in real bands and knew the ropes on cold-calling bars to line up gigs.

In our own ways, Schmidty, Kev, and I took the band equally seriously. Schmidty played the tortured artist, drinking more during the weekdays, while Kev took to writing lyrics during his classes when he should have been listening to the downfall of Rome. I slowly replaced my worn Levis and T-shirts with skinny black jeans and multicolored button-down shirts. I sold back my textbooks from fall quarter and bought a thin, hot-pink leather tie for thirty-four dollars, more than I'd spent on a single item of clothing in my life. We began practicing twice a week in Pauly's parents' garage—usually Monday nights after a weekend show to see what we could improve, and Thursdays to gear up for the next—depending on our class schedules, which we were beginning to see as suggestions rather than requirements.

We wouldn't drive over fifty miles unless the kitty was three hundred bucks, and now that we were pulling down between two hundred and eight hundred most weekends, depending on how many shows we hit, Schmidty and I quit our cafeteria jobs. We were recognized around our side of Milwaukee—at Jeepers Café near campus, and Arnold's Liquor where people knew the bar scene. A girl I'd never met stopped me at the Gas N Go and asked me for my autograph. It was early evening on a Saturday, and I was decked out for a show—the hot-pink skinny tie and my ever-present sunglasses that I wore every day, in class or outside, even in the dull gray of early spring. She stood chomping her gum with her receipt and a pen extended, but I wasn't sure how she knew me or who she thought I was—Joey Kowalski from The Carz or the real Ric Ocasek. I didn't know whose signature she wanted, how to sign my own name.

By April we were pulling down over a thousand most weeks, the number of gigs rising as people prepared for the end of the semester, the return to their regular lives. We were hoping to shore up enough money to get an apartment together on the East Side rather than return home to our parents' houses—the ranch-style homes of our youth—but split five ways, a thousand wasn't very much, not even in the eighties.

We spent our last weekend in the Bartock's garage rocking out to *Candy-O*, talking about our plans for the summer. I was unsure how I'd make it three months in South Side where no one knew me as something special, just Joey Kowalski, Carol and Stevie's son, the first punk in the family to go to college thanks to student loans, but who was fucking it up with a 1.8 GPA. Back home my first night my dad pointed his fork at me across the dinner table and said, "Take off those glasses. You look like a goddamn queer." I resumed my job as assistant to the assistant groundskeeper and within two weeks had lost my white pallor, the trademark of Ric Ocasek.

Katie showed up at the golf course a few weeks later—her college was on quarters and went into June—and she found me on the third hole aerating the edge of the green. "Hey," she said, a hand shading her eyes. "You busy?"

Her sophomore year hadn't been quite what she anticipated either, and spring quarter she'd failed more classes than she passed, landing on academic probation. I told her she was in good company and that maybe it was true some of us weren't cut out for college, that we were meant for the rock and roll life. Or maybe it was true what our parents said: that we just didn't try hard enough. Either way, I listened to every word she said, the consonants and vowels dripping from her mouth, the love of my young life. I put aside everything I'd learned the previous year about being cool and aloof and told her I loved her, that I'd never stopped loving her and never would. Maybe it was just that we were stuck in the rut of being home and being nothing, just back to ourselves, but it felt good and right to be there.

I spent the rest of the summer with Katie—eating peaches on her parents' porch, watching fireworks at Veterans Park, drinking tap beer at Cutty's on Fifth while our parents were two doors down at Taggarts. Their jukebox played Joni Mitchell and Bob Dylan while ours blared Springsteen and the E Street Band. When I'd slip in a quarter and The Cars would come rumbling over the speakers, it felt like another man singing our songs, and I had to remind myself it was—that I had never been, nor would I ever be, Ric Ocasek.

Katie and I spent our last Saturday together at Lake Michigan, her in a black polka-dot bikini with red bows tied on the sides of her hips. In the two months she'd been back she'd turned from neon pop to a punkier look, heavy eyeliner around her eyes and a darkish-purple lipstick, when last summer she'd worn no makeup at all. "We need to talk," she started, and even without the words that followed I knew we were unraveling.

By the time I returned to school that fall, The Cars were starting to wane. They hadn't had a radio hit in months, and in the eighties—a decade of instant gratification and short memory—that didn't cut it. The guys and I met to practice a few times but it wasn't the same; Schmidty had a hard time showing up sober, while Kev said he was sick of playing other people's music. He'd written some of his own songs over the summer and recorded them instrument by instrument on a cassette tape, which we attempted to air-play, but the songs were darker than we were used to, the sounds deep and mysterious. The Carz broke up right before 1987, and The Cars were just a year behind. Without the band between us, Schmidty, Kev, and I drifted apart, although we'd been good friends before all that came along. I'd see Kev on campus every now and again and we'd either nod or avoid eye contact, and Schmidty I'd see down at Liquor Lyles where he now bounced on the weekends. At the door I'd twist my hand by my right eye as if I were unscrewing my head and he'd grunt a laugh. No matter how busy, he'd always move me to the front of the line.

Even by 1992—the year I graduated college after a brief hiatus at Schlitz that had me hightailing it back to school with some determination—telling people about The Carz seemed like a joke, the days of yore when I was in an air band. Grunge was on its way in, where the point was to be as authentic as possible. "An air band!" a girl would eventually shriek and ask me to tell the story, how it happened, and why we went with The Cars. The band had turned into a footnote to eighties music, when for us, for a year, they were everything rock and roll meant: rebellion, individuality, the ugly guy who gets the girl. I tell Patty's friends about the wooden guitars we added after the New Year's gig, but not that Kevin's brother sweated over his jigsaw in his basement, the angry footsteps of his wife pounding the linoleum above in a two-bedroom house they couldn't afford. I tell them we thought what we were doing mattered, and that mattering wasn't something we were used to on our side of the tracks in Milwaukee. I tell them how at one point we even considered buying a tour bus—Schmidty knew a guy who knew a guy who had an abandoned school bus in his yard and would sell it for four hundred bucks, and we went so far as to design a logo for the side. I tell them the deal fell through because of some legal issues, but what I don't say is that for months I fell asleep thinking of that bus and how I'd pull it into Katie's driveway and she'd climb on board—because I know, for them, that's taking the joke too far.

After the story—the dining room table littered with dessert plates, half-filled cups of decaf, wine glasses with the last drop of red spread like an inkblot at the bottom—Patty leans into my chest, a contented look on her face. Everyone has laughed at the right places, sighed where appropriate, and the women have added stories of their own eighties fiascos, the men disappointed they never thought of such an easy way to impress girls. But as sometimes happens when I tell the story, the telling of it has made me sad. Katie was right: I'm romantic and nostalgic to a fault.

Nimisha picks up her cell phone and looks at the screen. "We need to get going. We told the babysitter we'd be home an hour ago." She smiles at me. "But how could we leave in the middle of a story like that?"

"Impossible," Patty agrees. We gather everyone's coats from the spare bedroom and see our guests to the door. Each woman kisses Patty on the cheek, and tells her they can't remember when they've had so much fun at a dinner party, when they've met such an interesting set of people. Ursula says she'll call Pats tomorrow and raises her eyebrows in C.J.'s direction as he struggles to find the armhole of his jacket.

Patty is flushed from wine and sleepiness, and as she closes the front door, she's careful to leave the light on until the last car drives away. "I'll never get tired of that story," she says. I want to ask her why, then, she won't make it permanent, move into this house and listen to my stories for the rest of her life. We Saran Wrap the leftovers and rinse out the wine glasses but leave the bulk of the cleaning for the morning. Upstairs Patty changes into a T-shirt and a pair of my boxers then sits on the bed and folds her legs like a pretzel, the small dolphin tattoo on her ankle exposed. Patty's a few years younger than I am, went to college in the nineties, and now she covers the tattoo with a Band-Aid when she wears sandals to work in the summer. Each decade has its mistakes, some more permanent than others. I watch as she rubs lotion absent-mindedly into her elbows, each elbow cupped in the opposite palm. I would have married Patty the month I met her, but she tells me she's not ready to get into all that again, that there's too much at stake with Cass, but Cass is one of the reasons I'd do it. That kid's a national treasure. A few months ago we were cleaning out the garage while Patty worked her one Saturday a month—just what a twelve-year-old kid wants to do on a Saturday morning, right? But she hardly complained, and it wasn't only because I promised her we'd head to the mall afterward so she could pick out a pair of earrings, as dangly as she wanted. In the garage we found one of the plywood guitars. "I thought I'd gotten rid of those years ago," I said, although I'm sure you know me well enough by now to know that isn't true. I told her about the band and how we were local celebrities in our neck of the woods, about the hours we spent practicing, and how it still wasn't enough to win Katie back. When I finished the story, Cass had tears in her eyes. "Joe," she said solemnly, "you're better off without her." Kids have no capacity for irony, and as such she's really the only one who understands the story, although it's not about Katie, not entirely.

Pats and I climb into bed. She holds up the remote, her way of asking if I want to watch *Law & Order*, and I say that's fine because I know she likes to have the TV on in the background when she falls asleep. Ric Ocasek's done some great work since the eighties—I've followed his career—but for all his musical genius, ended up the guy known for being married to the supermodel Paulina Porizkova. When they first started dating back in 1984 after meeting on the set of one of his videos, everyone said it wouldn't last, that they had nothing in common, that there was no way someone like her would stay with someone like him. His fans say it's sad his talent was usurped by his personal life, but talk about missing the point of a story. At the time of this telling, they've been together over twenty-five years.

Source Acknowledgments

These stories first appeared in slightly different form in the following publications: "The Good Neighbor" in *Prairie Schooner* 84, no. 2 (Summer 2010): 148–58; "Dog People" in *Colorado Review* 37, no. 1 (Spring 2010): 29–45; "I Don't Live in This Town" in the *Madison Review* 28, no. 1 (Fall 2006): 48–61; "The Summer of Cancer" in the *Florida Review* 34, no. 1 (Summer 2009): 37–44; "A Democrat in Nebraska" in *Lake Effect* 12 (Spring 2008): 47–60; "The Only Thing That Can Take You" in *Crazyhorse* 71 (Spring 2007): 134–44; and "All I Want Is You" published online in *Wag's Revue* no. 6 (Summer 2010).

In the Flyover Fiction Series

Ordinary Genius
Thomas Fox Averill

Jackalope Dreams
Mary Clearman Blew

*It's Not Going to Kill You, and
Other Stories*
Erin Flanagan

The Usual Mistakes
Erin Flanagan

Reconsidering Happiness: A Novel
Sherrie Flick

Twelfth and Race
Eric Goodman

The Floor of the Sky
Pamela Carter Joern

The Plain Sense of Things
Pamela Carter Joern

Stolen Horses
Dan O'Brien

Haven's Wake
Ladette Randolph

Because a Fire Was in My Head
Lynn Stegner

Bohemian Girl
Terese Svoboda

Tin God
Terese Svoboda

Another Burning Kingdom
Robert Vivian

Lamb Bright Saviors
Robert Vivian

The Mover of Bones
Robert Vivian

Water and Abandon
Robert Vivian

The Sacred White Turkey
Frances Washburn

Skin
Kellie Wells

To order or obtain more information on these or other University
of Nebraska Press titles, visit www.nebraskapress.unl.edu.

FLANA   CEN
Flanagan, Erin.
It's not going to kill you, and other
 stories /
CENTRAL LIBRARY
04/14